PUFFIN BOOKS

THE MOUSE AND HIS CHILD

Having once been set in motion, we cannot wind up our own clockwork again. But we can make toys whose stillness can be rewound to new motion, toys whose stillness is never final until the clockwork is destroyed. Clockwork toys are made in two tin halves that never fit exactly together, fastened with tin clasps that break if undone too often They keep what they are wound to keep, their little time, their little motion.

The mouse and his child, the actual toy that made me start writing novels, was made by the Schuco Spielwarenwerke of Nürnberg. They also manufactured a monkey who slowly and quietly beats a tin drum, a clown who bows a silent violin, a juggler who holds his hands apart while four coloured balls revolve on wires radiating from a shaft fixed in his breast. I don't know how many of them were made: thousands, probably. Each toy insisting on its one idea, its one action. Assembled with or without thought by human hands and eyes and minds that put, whether they wanted to or not, some yes or no, some why? or why not? into the toys. *Something* was put into them. Certainly there's more in those toys than clockwork. Posted all over the world they were, some to prosper, some to be smashed and thrown away, their active insistence spent.

What then is one to do on seeing a toy mouse father and mouse child who dance in a circle, the father swinging the child up and down more and more slowly as his spring unwinds? One pays attention, I think, and lets them tell the story they were wound to tell.

Russell Hoban

RUSSELL HOBAN

THE MOUSE
AND HIS CHILD

Pictures by Lillian Hoban

PUFFIN BOOKS
IN ASSOCIATION WITH FABER & FABER LTD

PUFFIN BOOKS

Published by the Penguin Group
Penguin Books Ltd, 27 Wrights Lane, London w8 5tz, England
Viking Penguin, a division of Penguin Books USA Inc.
375 Hudson Street, New York, New York 10014, USA
Penguin Books Australia Ltd, Ringwood, Victoria, Australia
Penguin Books Canada Ltd, 2801 John Street, Markham, Ontario, Canada l3r 1b4
Penguin Books (NZ) Ltd, 182–190 Wairau Road, Auckland 10, New Zealand

Penguin Books Ltd, Registered Offices: Harmondsworth, Middlesex, England

First published in the USA 1967
Published by Faber & Faber Ltd 1969
Published in Puffin Books 1976
13 15 17 19 20 18 16 14 12

The verse from the poem 'Leap Before You Look', which appears at the
beginning of the book, is from Collected Poetry of W. H. Auden, copyright 1945
by W. H. Auden. Reprinted by permission of Faber & Faber Ltd

Printed in England by Clays Ltd, St Ives plc
Set in Linotype Pilgrim

Author's Note

I am delighted to acknowledge my indebtedness to Ferdinand Monjo for his perceptive criticism and continuing encouragement through three years of work on this book; without him I think it might have taken ten.

These pages are dedicated to the memory of three fathers:
A. T. Hoban,
Edward Lewis Wallant,
and
Harvey Cushman, under whose Christmas tree I first saw the mouse and his child dance.

R.H.
February 1967

The sense of danger must not disappear:
The way is certainly both short and steep,
However gradual it looks from here;
Look if you like, but you will have to leap.

W. H. AUDEN

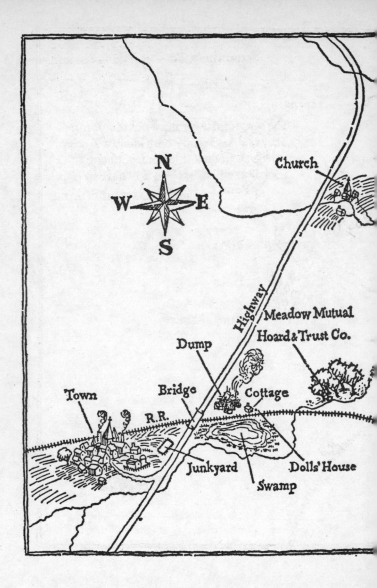

ONE

THE tramp was big and squarely built, and he walked with the rolling stride of the long road, his steps too big for the little streets of the little town. Shivering in his thin coat, he passed aimlessly through the crowd while rosy-faced Christmas shoppers quickened their steps and moved aside to give him room.

The sound of music made him stop at a toyshop where the door, continually swinging open and shut in a moving stream of people, jangled its bell and sent warm air and Christmas carols out into the street. 'Deck the halls with boughs of holly,' sang the loudspeakers in the shop, and the tramp smelled Christmas in the pine wreaths, in the bright paint and varnish, in the shining metal and fresh pasteboard of the new toys.

He put his face close to the window, and looking past the toys displayed there, peered into the shop. Under the wreaths and winking coloured lights a little train clattered through sparkling tunnels and over painted mountains on a green table, the tiny clacking of its wheels circling in and out of the music. Beyond it the shelves were packed with tin toys and wooden toys and plush toys – dolls, teddy bears, games and puzzles, fire engines and boats and wagons, and row on row of closed boxes, each printed with a fascinating picture of the toy it hid from sight.

On the counter, rising grandly above the heads of the children clustered before it, was a splendid dolls' house. It was very large and expensive, a full three stories high, and a marvel of its kind. The porches and balconies were elegant with scrollwork brackets, and the mansard roof with its dormers and cross gables was topped by tall brick chimneys and a handsome lookout. In front of the house stood a clock-work elephant wearing a purple head-cloth, and when the saleslady wound her up for the watching children, she walked slowly up and down, swinging her trunk and flapping her ears. Near the elephant a little tin seal balanced a red and yellow ball on her nose and kept it spinning while her reflection in the glass counter top smiled up at her and spun its own red and yellow ball.

As the tramp watched, the saleslady opened a box and took out two toy mice, a large one and a small one, who stood upright with outstretched arms and joined hands. They wore blue velveteen trousers and patent leather shoes, and they had glass-bead eyes, white thread whiskers, and black rubber tails. When the saleslady wound the key in the mouse father's back he danced in a circle, swinging his little son up off the counter and down again while the children laughed and reached out to touch them. Around and around they danced gravely, and more and more slowly as the spring unwound, until the mouse father came to a stop holding the child high in his upraised arms.

The saleslady, looking up as she wound the toy again, saw the tramp's whiskered, staring, face on the other side of the glass. She pursed her mouth and looked away, and the tramp turned from the window back to the street. The grey sky had begun to let down its snow, and the ragged man stood in the middle of the pavement while the soft flakes fell around him and the people quick-stepped past him.

Then, with his big broken shoes printing his footsteps in the fresh snow, he solemnly danced in a circle, swinging his empty arms up and down. A little black-and-white spotted dog trotting past stopped and sat down to look at him, and for a moment the man and the dog were the only two creatures on the street not moving in a fixed direction. People laughed, shook their heads, and hurried on. The tramp stopped with arms upraised. Then he lowered his head, jammed his hands into his pockets, and lurched away down the street, around a corner, and into the evening and the lamplight on the snow. The dog sniffed at his footprints, then trotted on where they led.

The store closed. The customers and clerks went home. The music was silent. The wreaths were dim, the shop was dark except for the dolls' house on the counter. Light streamed from all its windows out into the shadows around it, and the toys before it stood up silhouetted black and motionless as the hours slowly passed.

Then, 'Midnight!' said the old store clock. Its pendulum swung gleaming in the shadows as it counted twelve thin chimes into the silence, folded its hands together, and stared out through the dark window at the thick snow sifting through the light of the street lamp. Far away and muffled by the snow the town hall clock struck midnight with its deeper note.

'Where are we?' the mouse child asked his father. His voice was tiny in the stillness of the night.

'I don't know,' the father answered.

'*What* are we, Papa?'

'I don't know. We must wait and see.'

'What astonishing ignorance!' said the clockwork elephant. 'But of course you're new. I've been here such a long time that I'd forgotten how it was. Now, then,' she said, 'this place is a toyshop, and you are toy mice. People are going to come and buy you for children, because it's almost a time called Christmas.'

'Why haven't they bought you?' asked the little tin seal. 'How come you've stayed here so long?'

'It isn't quite the same for me, my dear,' replied the elephant. 'I'm part of the establishment, you see, and this is my house.'

The house was certainly grand enough for her, or indeed for anyone. The very cornices and carven brackets bespoke a residence of dignity and style, and the dolls never set foot

outside it. They had no need to; everything they could possibly want was there, from the covered platters and silver chafing dishes on the sideboard to the ebony grand piano among the potted ferns in the conservatory. No expense had been spared, and no detail was wanting. The house had rooms for every purpose, all opulently furnished and appropriately occupied: there were a piano-teacher doll and a young-lady-pupil doll in the conservatory, a nursemaid doll for the children dolls in the nursery, and a cook and butler doll in the kitchen. Interminable-weekend-guest dolls lay in all the guest room beds, sporting dolls played billiards in the billiard room, and a scholar doll in the library never ceased perusal of the book he held, although he kept in touch with the world by the hand he lightly rested on the globe that stood beside him. There was even an astronomer doll in the lookout observatory, who tirelessly aimed his little telescope at one of the automatic fire sprinklers in the ceiling of the shop. In the dining room, beneath a glittering chandelier, a party of lady and gentleman dolls sat perpetually around a table. Whatever the cook and butler might hope to serve them, they had never taken anything but tea, and that from empty cups, while plaster cakes and pastry, defying time, stood by the silver teapot on the white damask cloth.

It was the elephant's constant delight to watch that tea party through the window, and as the hostess she took great pride in the quality of her hospitality. 'Have another cup of tea,' she said to one of the ladies. 'Try a little pastry.'

'HIGH-SOCIETY SCANDAL, changing to cloudy, with a possibility of BARGAINS GALORE!' replied the lady. Her papier-mâché head being made of paste and newsprint, she always spoke in scraps of news and advertising, in whatever order they came to mind.

'Bucket seats,' remarked the gentleman next to her. 'Power steering optional. GOVERNMENT FALLS.'

The mouse child was still thinking of what the elephant had said before. 'What happens when they buy you?' he asked her.

'That, of course, is outside of my experience,' said the elephant, 'but I should think that one simply goes out into the world and does whatever one does. One dances or balances a ball, as the case may be.'

The child remembered the bitter wind that had blown in through the door, and the great staring face of the tramp at the window with the grey winter sky behind him. Now that sky was a silent darkness beyond the street lamp and the white flakes falling. The dolls' house was bright and warm; the teapot gleamed upon the dazzling cloth. 'I don't want to go out into the world,' he said.

'Obviously the child isn't properly brought up,' said the elephant to the gentleman doll nearest her. 'But then how could he be, poor thing, without a mother's guidance?'

'PRICES SLASHED,' said the gentleman. 'EVERY-THING MUST GO.'

'You're quite right,' said the elephant. 'Everything must, in one way or another, go. One does what one is wound to do. It is expected of me that I walk up and down in front of my house; it is expected of you that you drink tea. And it is expected of this young mouse that he go out into the world with his father and dance in a circle.'

'But I don't want to,' said the mouse child, and he began to cry. It was an odd, little, tinny, rasping, sound, and father and son both rattled with it.

'There, there,' said the father, 'don't cry. Please don't.' Toys all around the shop were listening. 'He'd better stop that,' they said.

It was the clock that spoke next, startling them with his flat brass voice. 'I might remind you of the rules of clock-work,' he said. 'No talking before midnight and after dawn, and no crying on the job.'

'He's not on the job,' said the seal. 'We're on our own time now.'

'Toys that cry on their own time sometimes cry on the job,' said the clock, 'and no good ever comes of it. A word to the wise.'

'Do be quiet,' said the elephant to the mouse child. 'I'll sing you a lullaby. Pay attention now.' The mouse child stopped crying, and listened while the elephant sang:

> Hush, hush, little plush,
> Mama's near you through the night.
> Hush, hush, little plush,
> Everything will be all right.

'Are you my mama?' asked the child. He had no idea what a mama might be, but he knew at once that he needed one badly.

'Good heavens!' said the elephant. 'Of course I'm not your mama. I was simply singing words I once heard a large teddy bear sing to a small one.'

'Will you *be* my mama,' said the child, 'and will you sing to me all the time? And can we all stay here together and live in the beautiful house where the party is and not go out into the world?'

'Certainly not!' snorted the elephant. 'Really,' she said to the gentleman doll, 'this is intolerable. One is polite to the transient element on the counter, and see what comes of it.'

'Twenty-one-inch colour television,' offered the gentleman. 'Nagging backaches and muscle tension. A HEART-WARMING LOVE STORY THE WHOLE FAMILY WILL ENJOY.'

'You're an idiot,' snapped the elephant, and no one on the counter said another word for the rest of the night. Outside the window the snowflakes whirled into the lamplight and out into the darkness again; inside the shop the clock ticked slowly through the slow dim hours, and the tea party in the dolls' house silently continued.

The next day the mouse and his child were sold. While the elephant walked back and forth and the seal balanced her ball and the ladies and gentlemen sat over their teacups, the father and son were put into a box, wrapped up, and carried off.

They came out of their wrappings to find the store gone and themselves under a Christmas tree with other toys around them. The tree was hung with lights and angels, and smelled of the pine woods. The fire crackled and sang on the hearth, and the children curled up on the rug with the family cat to watch the toys perform. A furry white rabbit struck his cymbals together with a tiny clash; a tin monkey played 'La Golondrina' on a little violin; a tin bird pecked steadily at the floor. And the mouse and his child danced.

Presents in bright wrappings were piled all round them, but the windup toys were not presents for the children; the grown-ups brought them down from the attic every year with the Christmas ornaments, and every year after Christmas they were packed away again. 'You may look at them,' said the grown-ups to the children, 'but we must wind them for you. Then they will not be broken, and we can enjoy them for many Christmases.'

So the mouse and his child danced under the tree every evening, and every night when the family was asleep they talked with the other toys. The monkey complained of being made to play the same tune over and over on a cheap fiddle; the bird complained of having to peck at a bare floor; the rabbit complained that there was no meaning in his cymbals. And soon the mouse and his child complained of the futility of dancing in an endless circle that led nowhere.

Every evening the toys performed, and every day the pine tree shed more needles on the floor around them until Christmas was gone. Then the tree was thrown out and the toys were packed off to the attic with the ornaments. There they lay jumbled in a box together, in the warm, sharp, dry smell of the attic beams and the dim light of the clouded, cobwebbed windows. Through long days and nights they listened to the rain on the roof and the wind in the trees, but the sound of the living room clock striking midnight could not reach them; they never had permission to speak at all, and they lay in silence until another year had passed and they stood once more beneath the tree.

So it was that four Christmases came and went, until there came a fifth Christmas that was different from the others.

*

'Wind up the toys for us!' said the children as they lay on the rug by the fire and leaned their cheeks on their hands.

When the mouse father was wound up, he danced in a circle as he always did, swinging the child up and down. The room, the tree, and the faces in the firelight whirled past the child as always, but this time he saw something new: among the other presents stood a dolls' house, a little one-room affair with a red-brick pattern printed on its fibreboard walls.

As the mouse child danced by with his father, he looked through the dolls' house window and saw a very small teddy bear and a pink china baby doll sitting at a table on which was a tea set bigger than both of them. Around and around the mouse child danced, rising and falling as his father swung him up and down, while the little tea party in the window circled past him.

How far away that other dolls' house seemed now! How far away that other tea party with its elegant ladies and gentlemen, and the elephant he had wanted for a mama! The mouse child was on the job and he knew it, but he began to cry.

No one noticed his outbreak but the family cat. She had grown used to the mechanical toys and no longer paid any attention to them, but the strange little sound of the mouse child's sobbing startled and upset her. She dabbed at the toy, arched her back, jumped suddenly sidewise, and leaping on to a table, knocked over a heavy vase of flowers. It fell with a crash, landing squarely on the mouse and his child. The vase was shattered to bits, and the toy was smashed.

*

Early the next morning the tramp came through the town, as he did each winter. With the little dog still at his heels he walked the snowy street past the house where the children and the grown-ups lived. He looked into the dust-bin to see what he might be able to use, took an empty coffee can and a bundle of newspapers, and went back to the junkyard where he had slept the night before in a wrecked car. Only then did he find the mouse and his child inside the papers, crushed almost flat but still holding fast to each other.

The tramp looked at the battered wrecks around him in the cold, clear sunlight. He looked down at himself in his ragged clothes. Then he sat down in the car he had slept in, and reached into his pocket for a little screwdriver. While the dog watched quietly, he took the mouse and his child apart to see if he could make them dance again. The junk-yard lay silent, its wrecks upheaved like rusty islands in the sparkling snow; the only sounds were the bells of Christmas ringing in the town and the cawing of some crows, hoarse and sharp in the cold air.

All that day the tramp sat in the junkyard labouring over the broken toy, stopping only to eat some bread and meat that he took from his pocket and shared with the dog. He was able to bend the tin bodies almost back into their original shapes, but he had a great deal of trouble with the clock-work motor. When he wound it up, the mechanism jammed, and in trying to clear it he broke some of the little cogs and bars that had made the mouse father dance in a circle and swing the child up and down. The tramp removed those parts and put the toy together as well as he could. Their patent leather shoes had been lost in the dust-bin; their blue velveteen trousers hung wrinkled and awry; their fur had come unglued in several places, but the mouse and his child were whole again.

Now when it was wound up the motor worked without jamming, but the mouse and his child danced no more. The father, his legs somewhat bent, lurched straight ahead with a rolling stride, pushing the child backwards before him. The little dog sat and watched them with his head cocked to one side. The ragged man smiled and threw away the leftover parts. Then he put the toy in his pocket and walked out to the highway.

High on a ridge above the town where snowy fields sloped off on either side, the road crossed a bridge over the railway tracks, went past the town rubbish dump, and stretched away to the horizon. The tramp set the mouse and his child down at the edge of the road and wound up the father.

'Be tramps,' he said, and turned and walked away with the dog at his heels.

TWO

THE mouse father walked forward on to the bridge, pushing the child backwards before him until his motor ran down and he could move no farther. Trains rumbled and shrieked on the tracks below. Cars and trucks shook the bridge as they roared past and vanished in the distance while father and son stood trembling.

The afternoon wore on towards evening, and the broken glass and mica of the roadside glittered in the last, low sunlight of the day. The snowy fields glowed briefly and went dark. At the dump the fires of burning rubbish smouldered, red and smoky in the dusk. The bridge lights went on, and beyond their unearthly blue glare the highway lamps spaced out the twilight to the dark horizon. A gibbous moon stared crookedly down from the cold sky until it was blotted out by clouds. Far away the clock on the town hall tolled the hours, and the mouse and his child waited in silence until they heard the twelve faint strokes of midnight.

'You see now where your crying has brought us,' said the father.

'I'm sorry, Papa,' said the child. 'I didn't mean to cry. I couldn't help it.'

The father looked thoughtfully into the night beyond the bridge, where red taillights diminished and white headlights continually approached. The wind was rising, and in the silences between the traffic, the girders of the bridge creaked with the cold. 'How strange it is to walk straight ahead!' he said.

'I walked backwards,' said the child, 'but I liked it better than dancing in a circle. What shall we do now?'

'Who knows?' said the father. 'There seems to be a good deal more to the world than the Christmas tree and the attic and the dust-bin. Anything at all might happen, I suppose.'

'But it won't,' said a soft voice close by. 'Not this evening, my lads.'

A large rat crept out of the shadows of the girders into the light of the overhead lamps, and stood up suddenly on his hind legs before the mouse and his child. He wore a greasy scrap of silk paisley tied with a dirty string in the manner of a dressing gown, and he smelled of darkness, of stale and mouldy things, and garbage. He was there all at once and with a look of tenure, as if he had been waiting always just beyond their field of vision, and once let in would never go away. In the eerie blue glare he peered beadily at father and son, and his eyes, as passing headlights came and went, flashed blank and red like two round tiny ruby mirrors. His whiskers quivered as his face came closer; he bared his yellow teeth and smiled, and a paw shot out to strike the mouse and his child a rattling blow that knocked them flat.

'Time to be moving along now,' said the rat. He set them on their feet, wound up the father, and guided them across the bridge and up the road towards the dump. As they walked below the highway lamps their shadows swung behind them, then before, then disappeared in darkness till the next dim circled light was reached.

'Where are you taking us?' asked the father.

'To a ball,' said the rat. 'To a jolly, jolly ball at the royal palace, where we shall all drink champagne and dance until dawn. How'll that be?' He laughed softly. His voice, half pleasant, half repellent, was oddly mild and persuasive.

'Are we really going to a palace?' asked the child.

'I don't think so,' said the father. 'He's teasing us.'

'Yes,' said the rat, 'I'm a dreadful tease – famous for my sense of humour. And here we are home again, safe and sound.'

They were off the highway now, and at the dump. Stumbling over snow-covered rubbish, they followed a path through a city of rats and other vermin, where little refuse fires tended by the inhabitants threw dancing shadows on the dirty snow. Tunnels and alleyways led through the rubbish to dark and filthy dwellings. Skulking figures watched them pass, and loud rat voices all around them quarrelled, cursed, and sang. The pathway widened as they went, and little hole-and-corner stalls with rat proprietors appeared.

'Orange peels – imported and domestic! Fancy moulds – green, white, and black!' cried a wizened little vendor with matted fur. 'Bacon grease, guaranteed two months old – some with egg scraps – going fast!' He beckoned to the dressing-gowned rat. 'How about some caviar, Manny?' he said. 'Hard as a rock. Not less than six weeks old. Very nice.'

Manny Rat fingered the caviar and handed it back. 'Haven't you got any of that imported treacle brittle?' he said. 'The kind that comes wrapped in red foil?'

'Next trip my buyer makes,' said the other. He winked at Manny Rat, then continued his chant. 'Orange peels! Bacon grease! Scented soaps! Library paste!'

As the mouse and his child stumbled on they heard thin and ragged voices singing:

> Who's that passing in the night?
> Foragers for Manny Rat!
> We grab first and we hold tight –
> Foragers for Manny Rat!

The voices trailed off wearily in groans and curses.

'Come on,' snarled someone, 'keep it moving, you!'

'My spring's gone,' came the tinny reply. 'See for yourself – one end of it's sticking out of my chest. I'm done!'

'No such luck,' said another tin voice as the unseen group passed out of earshot.

Manny Rat snickered, and pushed the mouse and his child along through an evil-smelling huddle of gambling dens, gaming booths, dancehalls and taverns, all crudely built of scraps of wood and cardboard boxes. The bonfires in the alleyways threw moving shadows of the revellers large on walls of open stalls; the dancehalls thumped and whistled savagely with tin-can drums, reed pipes, and matchbox banjos, while the dim light of candles through the doors and windows sent bobbing rat shapes dancing blackly on the snow. Farther off above the general din there rose the cracked voice of a windup carousel that played a waltz with many missing notes. Beyond the rubbish mountains and the fires wailed a passing freight, its wheels faintly clacking on the distant rails.

'Hurry, hurry! Step right up!' shouted a red and black sexton beetle at the entrance of an orange-crate theatre. The guttering flames of birthday-candle stubs behind him threw his frisking shadow on the snow ahead. The beetle wore a cape made from the fur of a woolly bear caterpillar, but he shivered nonetheless.

'A scientific exhibit!' he announced to passersby. 'An education for the whole family!' He drew aside a ragged curtain to disclose, lit by the fitful candles, a headless pink celluloid hula doll wearing the faded remnants of a cellophane grass skirt. Two cricket musicians, barely kept from freezing by a nest of dead grass in a glass jar, huddled together, too cold to chirp.

'I don't like this place, Papa,' whimpered the mouse child.

'Hush,' said the father. 'Crying won't help.'

'Observe her curious motion as she sways this way and that!' urged the beetle. He wound the key in the headless doll's back, and she jiggled listlessly while the candle flames sank in the wind. 'Let's go, boys!' he said, and kicked the cricket jar. The crickets chirped once and lapsed into silence. The beetle let the curtain fall. 'There's more inside!' he yelled. 'Step up and see the show!'

'How much have you taken in this evening?' asked Manny Rat.

'Very slow tonight,' said the sexton beetle. He showed him the small end of a salami and a dead sparrow half buried in the snow.

'We haven't been burying anything on the sly, have we?' said Manny Rat, taking the salami. 'We make sure Manny always gets his cut?'

'It's been a slow winter,' said the beetle. 'I'm doing the best I can. Honest.'

Manny Rat wound up the mouse father, and they left the midway and started up a slope on which the father and the child fell many times. 'Almost there, chaps,' he said. 'Then you can rest your clockwork for a bit before you resume your duties.'

The slope levelled off. They walked through a rusty bed-spring, around the skeleton of a baby carriage, and found themselves in a long, narrow space where empty beer cans, standing like elms at the entrance to a manor, made an avenue that led to the gutted and screenless cabinet of a long-dead television set, the residence of Manny Rat.

The mouse and his child, unwound, came to a stop, while their captor sat down on the edge of the hole where the television screen had been and ate his salami. As he looked up into the night, the massed clouds lifted to reveal the sky. The moon had set; the stars were sharp and clear. Low above the horizon wheeled Orion the Hunter, and near the luminous scattering of the Milky Way, in the Great Dog constellation, blazed Sirius, the brightest star of all. Manny Rat liked dark nights best; he grimaced at the stars and turned away.

Standing as he was on uneven ground, the child was tilted at such an angle that he too saw the Dog Star, beyond his father's shoulder. He had never looked up at the sky before; indeed, he had as yet seen little of the earth, and even that little was more frightening than he had imagined. At first the icy glitter of the far-off star was terrifying to him; he sensed a distance so vast as to reduce him to nothing. But as he looked and looked upon that steady burning he was comforted a little; if he was nothing, he thought, so also was this rat and all the dump. His father's hands were firm upon his, and he resolved to see what next the great world offered.

'What are you going to do with us?' the father asked Manny Rat. 'Why have you brought us here?'

Manny Rat ignored the question, and looked back over the trodden snow towards the far end of the beer-can avenue. The mouse and his child heard the singing again, and in the dim starlight they saw, dark against the snow, an ugly young rat tough driving a group of battered windup toys ahead of him. There were more than a dozen of them, all staggering under the weight of the bags they carried on their backs. They had been salvaged from the dump by Manny Rat and Ralphie, his assistant and rat-of-all-work, and whatever mobility they possessed was due to the mechanical skill of the two rats. Once they had been kicking donkeys, dancing bears, tumbling clowns, roaring lions, baaing goats – all manner of specialities were represented in the group – but few of them by now had all their faculties, and most of them had lost a limb or two along with fur and clothing, eyes and ears. All their trades and tricks were gone; the best that they could do was plod ahead when wound, and that not very well. They tottered up the avenue, led by a mouldy goat, both lame and blind, who with the others feebly sang:

> Who's that passing in the night?
> Foragers for Manny Rat!
> Make your move and take your bite
> After us, or stand and fight
>   Manny Rat!

The song faltered into silence as the foragers came to a stop at various points between the beer cans, those whose springs were not completely unwound being knocked down by Ralphie. The mouse and his child stared at the other toys, and the standing members of the group stared back in silence.

'Where'd they come from?' asked Ralphie, as he shuffled up to report to his master.

'I found them wandering on the road,' said Manny Rat, 'where they'd evidently straggled away from your squad. Aren't these a couple of your new recruits?'

'I don't think I ever seen them two before,' said Ralphie. 'But all them windups look alike to me anyhow. I never know whether I got the whole squad unless I count.' He leered at the mouse and his child. 'Wandering on the road, hey? Maybe their motor's too strong. Maybe I should work them over a little.'

'Never mind them for now,' said Manny Rat. 'I should very much like to know who it was I heard complaining a little while ago. Something about a broken spring, I believe.'

'Him,' said Ralphie, pointing to a one-eyed, three-legged donkey. 'He got a lot to say.'

'It's nothing,' said the frightened donkey as he heard Manny Rat approach his blind side. 'I've got plenty of work left in me. I was just feeling a little low – you know how it is.'

'You're not well,' said Manny Rat. 'I can see that easily. What you need is a long rest.' He picked up a heavy rock, lifted it high, and brought it down on the donkey's back, splitting him open like a walnut. 'Put his works in the spare-parts can,' said Manny Rat to Ralphie.

The young rat deftly removed the donkey's motor-and-leg assembly and dropped it into an empty tin can that stood near the mouse and his child. BONZO Dog Food said the white letters on the orange label, and below the name was a picture of a little black-and-white spotted dog, walking on his hind legs and wearing a chef's cap and an apron. The dog carried a tray on which there was another can of BONZO Dog Food, on the label of which another little black-and-white spotted dog, exactly the same but much smaller, was walking on his hind legs and carrying a tray on which there was another can of BONZO Dog Food, on the label of which another little black-and-white spotted dog, exactly the same but much smaller, was walking on his hind legs and carrying a tray on which there was another can of BONZO Dog Food, and so on until the dogs became too small for the eye to follow. The father stared at the can as the parts fell in with a melancholy clink; the child's back was to it.

'What about the rest of our gallant foragers?' said Manny Rat. 'Is anyone else not feeling well tonight?' No one answered. Some standing, some lying in the snow, they waited in silence, their rusty metal and mildewed plush glinting with frost.

Manny Rat turned to the mouse father. 'I can see by the way you stare that you have not been here before,' he said. 'Let me welcome you, then, to the dump, and to our happy band.' He came closer, and bared his slanting yellow teeth. 'Notice my teeth, if you will,' he said. 'Pretty, aren't they? They're the longest, strongest, sharpest teeth in the dump.' He swept his paw around the dark horizon. 'All this will belong to Manny Rat one day,' he said. 'I'll be the boss of the whole place. Is that so or isn't it, Ralphie!' He leaped suddenly at the young rat.

'You're the boss, Boss,' said Ralphie, stepping back quickly. 'Don't get excited.'

Smiling and rubbing his paws together, Manny Rat walked over to the silent squad of toys. 'What have we tonight?' he said.

Ralphie emptied the bags, heaping on the snow bread crusts, apple cores, partly-eaten pork chops, two or three unfinished lollipops, a rotten egg, half a can of anchovies, two marbles, a piece of red glass, and other choice gleanings of the local dust-bins. 'That's it,' he said. 'And I seen another busted up windup we could fix. It was over by that smashed-up folding table, towards the road.'

'Any treacle brittle?' said Manny Rat.

'The last I heard of was the other day,' said Ralphie. 'A couple of fellows pulled off a job at a grocery store. But after they got the treacle brittle they put it in the vault over at the Meadow Mutual Hoard and Trust Company.'

'Then don't hang around here, for heaven's sake,' said Manny Rat. 'Get over there and get it for me.'

'How?' said Ralphie. 'I don't even know where the vault is.'

'Listen carefully and remember what I tell you,' said Manny Rat. 'First you go into the bank and tell them you're thinking of renting a safe-deposit hole. Then they'll show you the vault.'

'They'll show me the vault,' repeated Ralphie.

'Then you say, "Thank you," ' Manny Rat continued, 'and you go outside and dig a tunnel into the vault. The ground there is sandy, and its easy digging, but you must be very careful not to come out where the guard is.'

'Where the guard is,' said Ralphie. 'I got it.'

'Then you get the treacle brittle and bring it back here,' said Manny Rat. 'What could be simpler? There may be more than you can carry,' he said, licking his lips. 'Take a windup with you. Hurry now, while the bank's still open — they close at dawn.'

The mouse father heard, and he knew that here, for the moment at least, was a way forward and out of the dump. He could not look beyond that, and did not attempt to. *Take us*, he thought; *take us*.

'These two look like good carriers,' said Ralphie. He hung a paper bag from the joined hands of the mouse and his child, and wound up the father. 'Let's go,' he said, and started them moving across the dirty snow that gleamed pale in the starlit beer-can avenue.

'We have seen murder committed tonight,' said the father to his son, 'and now we are to be thieves. But we must keep moving forward.'

'Let's knock off the chatter,' said Ralphie. 'I got a lot to think about.' He began to mutter to himself, rehearsing the words he would say at the bank, while he pushed the mouse and his child ahead of him into a black, malodorous tunnel that wound down through the refuse piles and out beyond the rubbish mountains to the far edge of the dump.

The narrow passage dipped and twisted and climbed, and the mouse and his child, constantly falling and being set on their feet again by Ralphie, trudged on until they emerged into the open night on a steep, snow-covered tin-can slope above the red glare of the rubbish fires. A pall of smoke drifted over a narrow path across the slope, and here they heard someone approaching and the chanting of a deep and melancholy voice.

'ARE YOUR EYES LOSING THEIR REDNESS?' boomed the voice. 'HAS THE SNAP GONE OUT OF YOUR TAIL? NATURE'S REMEDIES AND RESTORA-TIVES SOLD HERE. LOVE POTIONS AND MAGIC CHARMS.'

'Him and his magic charms!' said Ralphie. 'If the boss didn't think it'd bring bad luck, I'd charm *him*!'

'DREAMS INTERPRETED,' continued the chant. 'FORTUNES TOLD. TERRITORIES SURVEYED. WEDDINGS PERFORMED. MODERATE FEES.' Black against the luminous smoke, an odd and slowly hop-ping shape appeared. Passing alternately through darkness and light as the flames below it rose and fell, it came steadily up the path, and drawing closer, revealed itself to be a large bullfrog who wore an old and tattered woollen glove against the winter cold. His bulging eyes looked out from the opening in which a hand would ordinarily be inserted, his limbs stuck out through four frayed holes, and the empty woollen

fingers and thumb dragged behind him. A coin swung from a string around his neck; a little bag of travel provisions hung at his side; a matchbox was slung on his back, and it rattled with his stock of herbs, medicinal sundries, charms, and amulets as he hopped through the winter, alone of his kind while all the world of frogs slept safely in the mud.

'Good evening,' he said as Ralphie came towards him with the mouse and his child. The frog's golden eyes took on red glints from the fires as he fixed upon father and son a look of profound and penetrating observation. 'WHAT FOR-

TUNE AWAITS YOU?' he boomed. 'FROG LIFTS THE VEIL THAT HIDES THE FUTURE. CREDIT GIVEN ON FAVOURABLE READINGS.'

'Listen,' said Ralphie, 'you sold me a charm last summer.'

'Ah,' said Frog, 'I remember. It was the herb called High John the Conqueror, for success in love.'

'Well, it don't work,' said Ralphie. 'I rubbed it all over me like you said, and it give me such a smell that the girl I was after run off with another rat.'

'Which proves she was the wrong girl for you,' said Frog. 'That is one of the charm's wondrous properties – it shows which love is true and which is false. Come, let me tell your fortune. No charge.'

Ralphie held out a paw, and Frog looked into it. 'Ah!' he said. His eyes flashed red and gold as he stared from the rat's paw into his face.

'What do you see?' said Ralphie.

'A journey,' said Frog, having noted the bag carried by the mouse and his child, 'a long journey.'

'You're wrong there,' said Ralphie. 'It's a short one.'

'One never knows about journeys,' said Frog. 'It may seem long.'

'What else?' said Ralphie, and he smacked his lips as he thought of the treacle brittle.

'There'll be good eating,' said Frog. 'I see that very definitely.'

'Tell our fortune,' said the mouse child.

'Windups don't have no fortune to tell,' said Ralphie.

'Not so,' said Frog. 'The future is impartial, and Fortune smiles on whom she will.' He bent close to the child. 'Tell me,' he said, 'what do you want from the future?'

'I want to find the elephant,' said the child. 'I want her to be my mama, and I want the seal to be my sister, and I want us all to live in the beautiful house.'

'Good heavens!' exclaimed the father. This was the first he had heard of the elephant and the seal and the dolls' house since they had left the store five years ago.

'Let us see what time will bring,' said Frog. 'As your palm is not accessible for me to read, I shall use an ancient form of divination that was taught me by an oriental mantis.' Ralphie, well content to put off his errand at the bank, watched with interest as the frog unslung the matchbox from his back and took out a handful of sunflower seeds. Then he removed from his neck the coin that hung there, and tossing it and the seeds together, watched them fall to the snow. 'Now,' he said, as he wound up the father, 'you must walk through the design.'

Three times, directed on different angles by the fortune-teller, father and son walked through the seeds and changed their random pattern in the snow. Then, squatting heavy and still, Frog examined the disposition of coin and seeds, staring concentratedly at their new arrangement, while above him the floating red smoke of the rubbish fires intermittently obscured the stars. Ralphie leaned close, watching intently, and the mouse and his child, unwound, waited.

The frog, as far as he himself knew, had never accurately predicted the future in his entire life. He told fortunes for profit, just as he sold charms and cures, surveyed territories, and performed weddings. The weddings at least were legal, since he was a legitimate justice of the peace; the surveys were more or less exact; the cures occasionally healed; the charms worked as hard as their wearers; and in the matter of fortunes he had learned long ago to say whatever best suited the occasion and the customer. The mouse child wanted a family and a house, and Frog desired to please him; therefore he went through the motions of the oriental divination, preparing the while to see in the future a mama, a sister, and a beautiful house.

So the frog intended, but as he looked at the coin and the

36

seeds he found himself unable to speak the words he had planned. He had practised the seed and coin oracle many times, but never before had he experienced anything like what was happening to him now. All else beyond the pattern in the snow departed from his vision; his ears hummed, and other sounds all vanished, leaving him alone with the voice of his mind and the dark seeds dancing in the stillness of their mystic changes.

'You have broken the circle,' he said, 'and a straight line of great force emerges. Follow it.'

'Where?' asked the father.

Frog traced a line from seed to seed, and made an up-and-down gesture. 'Depths and heights,' he said, 'but the bottom is strangely close to the top.' He paused. 'The road is long,' he said, 'and very hard.'

'But where does the road take us?' asked the child.

Frog stared harder at the seeds, his golden eyes unfathomable. His yellow throat swelled, gleaming in the opening of his ragged glove. He seemed to grow large and remote in the starlight, and his voice was distant when he spoke: '*Low in the dark of summer, high in the winter light; a painful spring, a shattering fall, a scattering regathered. The enemy you flee at the beginning awaits you at the end.*' The words stopped, and the voice went quivering into silence. The child began to cry.

'That isn't much to look forward to, is it?' said the father. 'Can't you tell us more than that?'

'No,' said Frog. 'Nor can I even read the meaning of the words I spoke.' Now that the words had gone from him he seemed smaller, nervous and uneasy. There was silence for a moment. The rat, the frog, and the mouse and his child, lit by a sudden flaring of the flames below, stood out sharply against the darkness, motionless on the tin-can slope.

'Let's go,' said Ralphie, shivering as if he felt the chill of winter for the first time. 'Let's get to where we're going.' He wound up the father, and they started on their way out of the dump to the dark fields beyond it. Behind them on the narrow path the frog·picked up the coin and the seeds, and watched them out of sight.

*

In the beer-can avenue the battered windups of the forage squad stood and lay in silence where they had stopped, while their master paced among them thinking treacle-brittle thoughts. The sky had clouded over again, and Manny Rat felt better with the stars out of sight. He looked towards the fires beyond the rubbish mountains, and sniffed the smoke complacently. Then, humming a little tune, he passed through the ranks of his silent slaves and went off to look for the windup Ralphie had told him about.

He found her near the wreckage of a bridge table, close to the highway. The purple headcloth was gone, her gray plush was black with rot, one eye and one ear were missing; but still the elephant maintained an air of monumental dignity.

How she had suffered! She who had thought herself a lady of property, secure in her high place – she had been sold like any common toy, while the gentlemen and ladies in the dolls' house never so much as looked up from their teacups. The house itself, *her* house, as she had always believed, had been cut off abruptly from her sight as the tissue paper closed about her head, and thus her world departed, and reality was thrust upon her.

She had been taken to a house much grander than the one on the counter, and there she had endured what toys endure. She had been smeared with jam and worried by the dog, she had been sat upon, and she had been dropped. She had been made to pull wagons, had been shot at by toy cannons, and had been left out in the rain until her works had rusted fast and she was thrown away. Still she endured, and deep within her tin there blazed a spirit that would not be quenched. Though the heavens should fall, she knew that justice one day would be done. That day, and that day only, was what she lived for: to pace again with swinging trunk beside the windows of the mansion that was hers; to know again the stately mode of life that was her due. In the meantime, here was a rat to be encountered, and he should be confronted firmly, as she had met all adversity thus far.

'Good evening, madam,' said Manny Rat. 'Do we find ourselves quite worn out and thrown away? Do we lie here, lonely in the wintry waste, and rot? The pity of it!'

The elephant said nothing.

'Be of good cheer,' said Manny Rat. 'Rejoice! Help is at hand!'

Still the elephant preserved her silence.

'Surely you can speak,' said Manny Rat. 'You have heard the striking of the town hall clock, and the hour is long past midnight.'

'We have not been introduced,' murmured the elephant almost inaudibly, as if she hoped to create the illusion that the words had not actually come from her.

'Ah, but we shall be!' said Manny Rat. 'We shall become, moreover, close friends and intimate associates.' He tried the elephant's key, but could not turn it. The spring was tightly wound and thick with rust. 'What better introduction could there be,' he said, 'than to take you apart and repair you so you can work for me?' He produced a rusty beer-can opener from within his robe and undid the tin clasps that held the elephant together.

'Nothing more to say, madam?' he asked as he pried apart the two halves of her tin body. 'Not so much as a how-do-you-do?'

But the elephant was silent. She had fainted.

*

The sky was beginning to pale, and the air was sharp with morning as Ralphie and the mouse and his child came through the woods along a path to the Meadow Mutual Hoard and Trust Company, an earthen bank beside a stream. There were many tracks in the snow, and following these, they went through the entrance between the roots of a great sycamore tree.

The interior of the bank was chill and dim and hushed; the acorn-cup tallow lamps did little more than cast their own shadows and catch the glint of frost and mica on the earth walls. In the half-light a drowsy chipmunk teller looked up from the sunflower seeds he was counting as the rat walked in with the mouse and his child. The father pushed the son up to the rock behind which the chipmunk sat, then stood treading the ground until his spring unwound. The chipmunk looked at the paper bag they carried, then at Ralphie, and he felt for the alarm twig with his foot.

'Um yes,' he said. 'May I help you?'

Ralphie squinted cautiously into the shadows around him, saw no guards, and at once forgot everything Manny Rat had told him. 'All right,' he said, snarling and showing his teeth, 'this is a stickup. Take me to the vault.'

'Um yes, sir!' said the chipmunk, stepping hard on the alarm twig as he spoke. The twig passed through a hole in the dirt wall behind him, and its other end vibrated against the snout of the badger guard who was dozing behind the stone that was the door of the vault. The badger woke up and smiled.

'This way, please,' said the chipmunk. Ralphie wound up the mouse father, and they went through a short tunnel to where the stone blocked the opening of the vault. 'Here is the vault,' said the chipmunk.

'Well, open it up,' said Ralphie.

'Um certainly,' said the chipmunk. He moved the stone

and stepped out of the way as Ralphie rushed into the waiting jaws of the badger, who ate him up.

'Them city fellows ain't much at robbing banks,' chuckled the badger when he had finished, 'but they're good eating. Young fellows nowadays, they don't know how to pull a job. All they know is hurry, hurry, hurry.' He picked his teeth with a sliver of bone. 'What about them other two?' he asked the chipmunk.

The chipmunk looked back through the tunnel and out past the entrance of the bank. The mouse and his child, spun about by the violence of Ralphie's rush into the vault, had stumbled out of the Meadow Mutual Hoard and Trust Company into the blue dawn, leaving their paper bag behind them. The chipmunk watched them walk down the path until they bumped into a rock and fell over. He shook his head. 'Whatever they are, they're harmless,' he said. 'Let them go.'

The mouse and his child lay in the snow where they had fallen, rattling with tinny, squeaking laughter. 'Skreep, skreep, skreep!' laughed the father. 'The frog was right – Ralphie *did* go on a long journey.'

'Skreek, skreek!' laughed the child. 'There was good eating too, for the badger! Skreek!'

'Seven o'clock!' called the clock on the steeple of the church across the meadow as it struck the hour.

'Listen!' said the father as he heard it. 'It's time for silence. Skreep!' And he began laughing all over again.

'If it's time for silence, how is it that we're still talking, Papa?' giggled the child.

'You've already broken one of the clockwork rules by crying on the job,' said the father, 'so we might as well break the other one too, and have done with it.'

'But I've often tried to speak after dawn,' said the child, 'and I never could till now. I wonder how it happened?'

41

'Perhaps your laughter freed you from the ancient clock-work laws,' said a deep voice, and the bullfrog fortune-teller hopped out from behind a tree. In the daylight he seemed smaller than he had at night, and much of his mystery was gone. He was not a young frog; the glove he wore was shabby. In the cold light of morning he could be clearly seen for what he was: an old, eccentric traveller, neither respect-able nor reliable, hung with odd parcels, tricked out with a swinging coin, and plying his trade where chance might take him. He set the mouse and his child on their feet and con-sidered them thoughtfully. 'I have never heard a toy laugh before,' he said.

'Did you see what happened?' said the father, and he told the frog about the attempted bank robbery.

'A rash youth, Ralphie,' said Frog. 'He had no patience, poor boy! For once I read the future truly, and it came with fearful swiftness. But are you not curious about my presence here?'

'Why are you here?' asked the child.

'Because I followed you,' said Frog. 'Something draws me to you, and in the seeds I saw your fate and mine bound inextricably together. I said nothing at the time – I was afraid. There were dark and fearful things in that design, and unknown perils that can only be revealed by time.' He shook his head, and the coin swung like a pendulum from the string around his neck.

'Are you still afraid?' asked the father.

'Utterly,' said Frog. 'Do you choose to go ahead?'

'There is no going back,' said the father; 'we cannot dance in circles any more. Will you be our friend, and travel with us?'

'Be my uncle,' said the child. 'Be my Uncle Frog.'

'Ah!' said Frog. 'I had better make no promises; I am at best an infirm vessel. Do not expect too much. I will be your friend and uncle for as long as our destined roads may lie together; more than that I cannot say.' He gestured towards the snowy meadow that sparkled in the sunlight beyond the trees ahead, and pointed back along the shadowy pathway they had taken to the bank. 'Which shall it be?' he said. 'Towards the town, or out into the open country?'

'Maybe we could look for the elephant and the seal and the dolls' house that used to be in the store with us,' said the child. 'Couldn't we, Papa?'

'What in the world for?' said the father.

'So we can have a family and be cosy,' answered the child.

'To begin with,' said the father, 'I cannot imagine myself being cosy with that elephant. But, putting that aside for the moment, the whole idea of such a quest is impossible. Despite what she said, she and the dolls' house were very likely for sale just as we and the seal were, and by now they might be anywhere at all. It would be hopeless to attempt to find any of them.'

'She sang me a lullaby,' said the child.

'Really,' said the father, 'this is absurd.'

'I want the elephant to be my mama and I want the seal to be my sister and I want to live in the beautiful house,' the child insisted.

'What is all this talk of elephants and seals?' asked Frog.

'It's nonsense,' said the father, 'and yet it's not the child's fault. Our motor is in me. He fills the empty space inside himself with foolish dreams that cannot possibly come true.'

'Not so very foolish, perhaps,' said Frog. 'This seal, was she made of tin, and black and shiny? Did she have a small platform on her nose that revolved while a sparrow performed acrobatic tricks on it?'

'No,' said the father. 'She had a red and yellow ball on her nose.'

'She could have lost the ball,' said the child. 'Maybe she

does have a platform on her nose now. Where is the seal you saw?' he asked Frog.

'I don't know where she is now,' said Frog. 'But two years ago she was with a travelling theatrical troupe that comes to the pine woods every year.'

'If Uncle Frog could take us there, maybe we could find the seal,' said the mouse child to his father, 'and then we could all look for the elephant together.'

'Finding the elephant would be as pointless as looking for her,' said the father. 'But since I cannot convince you of that, we might just as well travel to the pine woods as anywhere else. At any rate we shall see something of the world.'

'Very well,' said Frog. 'On to the pine woods.'

'EXTRA!' screamed a raucous voice above them as a bluejay flashed by in the sunlight. 'RAT SLAIN IN BANK HOLDUP ATTEMPT. WINDUPS FLEE WITH GET-AWAY FROG. LATE SCORES: WOODMICE LEAD MEADOW TEAM IN ACORN BOWLING. VOLES IDLE.'

'So it begins,' said Frog. 'For good or ill, you have come out into the world, and the world has taken notice.'

'A long, hard road,' said the father to Frog. 'That was what you saw ahead for us, was it not?'

'All roads, whether long or short, are hard,' said Frog. 'Come, you have begun your journey, and all else necessarily follows from that act. Be of good cheer. The sun is bright. The sky is blue. The world lies before you.'

The father saw the brightness of the meadow through the dark trees. Two crows, sharp against the sky, sailed over it on broad, black wings, and he thought of how many steps it would take him to traverse the same distance. His spring tightened as the frog wound him; his motor buzzed, and he pushed his son ahead.

Behind them in the shadows of the trees stretched the double tracks of tin feet and the odd prints left by Frog's trailing woollen fingers. And bending over the trail in the snow was a figure clothed in a greasy scrap of silk paisley tied with a dirty string. The clockwork elephant followed, with two empty paper bags slung on her back. The planner of the bank robbery, growing doubtful of Ralphie's prompt return, had thought it prudent to come out to meet him and collect the booty.

' "Rat slain in bank holdup attempt," ' said Manny Rat. 'That idiot Ralphie! I suppose that means no treacle brittle for me. And those wretched windups have gone off with the frog as if their single purpose were to make a fool of me. Now I'll be the laughing-stock of the whole dump unless I find them and smash them!'

THREE

'Midnight!' rang the clock on the steeple of the church across the meadow. 'Twelve o'clock and all's peaceful here. Sleep well!'

Out of the light of the moon that floated clear in a cloudless sky, Frog paused under the trees that bordered the meadow. He turned to look back anxiously over the snow behind them, then faced forward again, listening. The mouse and his child walked on a little way, then stopped, unwound. 'What's the matter?' asked the child.

'I hear something up ahead,' said Frog. 'And Manny Rat is close behind us. I've seen him dodging in and out of the trees. If he catches us, I fear our friendship may not survive the encounter.'

'I hear something now,' said the child. It was a far-off, ghostly whistling, and the rhythmic whisper of a distant drum.

'Whatever it is,' said Frog, 'it can scarcely be worse than Manny Rat in his present mood. Let us press on.' He wound up the father, and hopped beside him and the child towards the sound of the drum and the whistling that now drew closer.

In the shadows of the trees ahead a green light, pale and dim, glimmered and was gone. Then it glimmered again. 'Fox fire beacon,' said Frog. He stopped, and knocked the mouse and his child down to stop them too. 'I've seen those before,' he said, 'and I've smelled that same musky scent I smell now. What's in front of us is . . .' He leaped aside as a wood mouse bolted past, dragging her children with her.

'War!' she cried.

The drumming grew fierce and louder, and the whistling could now be recognized as the shrill singing of piercing little voices accompanied by a reed fife:

> Onward, shrews, for territory!
> Victory crown our might!
> Onward, shrews, for fame and glory!
> Heroes, to the fight!

'What are shrews?' asked the child.

'They look something like mice,' said Frog; 'but they're short-tailed, sharper-nosed, and smaller – very little and very bloodthirsty. They eat constantly, and when they have a war they eat even more.' The mouse father's motor having run down, Frog stood him and the child on their feet again. The band of shrews was less than a hundred yards away, and the scout who had signalled with the phosphorescent wood moved off to join them. Frog watched the fox fire bobbing dimly, growing smaller in the distance.

'Their eyesight's very poor,' he said; 'they haven't seen us yet. Perhaps they'll go away, and just as well. They're a commissary company, I think, after rations. That's why the mouse was running so hard. In any case, they don't eat tin.'

'Do they eat frogs?' asked the child.

'When they catch them,' Frog replied.

The shrews moved into the moonlight, and the child, looking beyond his father's shoulder, saw the little company, spiky with the tiny spears they carried, clustered black against the snow. The singing had stopped, but the rolling beat of the nutshell drum and the piping of the reed fife continued while the scout made his report.

'Those spears have poisoned tips,' said Frog.

'Be careful,' said the child. 'Don't go any closer.'

'There's no going back, either,' said Frog. 'Here's Manny Rat.'

'Good evening!' called Manny Rat in a hoarse whisper. He had left the elephant in the brush behind him, the better to come upon his quarry in silence. 'Are we doubtful of the future?' he said. 'Do we wonder which way to turn?'

Frog, remembering his promise to travel with the mouse and his child for as long as their destined roads might lie together, decided that those roads must now diverge. Friendship was a noble thing, but life was sweet. Therefore he hopped out of the shadows to meet Manny Rat, hoping to find some soft answer that would turn away his anger from himself at least.

Manny Rat hesitated. The frog was utterly helpless against him, yet the rat became uneasy. He had always feared the fortune-teller a little; he felt him to be not only a prophet of good or bad luck, but its active agent as well. He drew nearer, and staring past the frog, he saw the mouse child staring back at him, the night sky mirrored in his glass-bead eyes. Manny Rat felt himself by some strange magnetism drawn to the father and the son, felt that something was wanted of him, forgot almost that he was there to smash them. He shook his head and picked up a rock. 'Step aside, Frog,' he said; 'I'm going to smash your friends.'

Frog, racking his brain for some way of placating Manny Rat, acted on a sudden impulse. 'Let me read your future,' he said.

Manny Rat held out his palm and laughed. 'Go ahead,' he said. 'I may very well be the only member of the present company that has one.'

Smiling, the frog approached, but he never took the rat's extended paw, nor did he speak the fair words he was shaping. He found himself looking into Manny Rat's eyes, and other words, obscure and cryptic, came into the fortune-teller's mind; against his will his broad mouth opened, and he spoke them: '*A dog shall rise*,' he said; '*a rat shall fall*.'

Manny Rat leaped back as if he had been struck. 'What's that supposed to mean?' he snarled.

Frog had no idea of what those words meant, nor did he care. He wished heartily that he had never set eyes upon the mouse and his child as his mouth opened again and he heard, as from a distance, his voice repeat, '*A dog shall rise; a rat shall fall*.'

'That may be,' said Manny Rat, his fears forgotten in his rage, 'but you'll fall first. You and your windup friends will finish up together. I'm going to tear your throat out.'

'Of course,' said Frog. 'Why not?' He nodded sadly, then turned his back on Manny Rat and looked towards the shrews as they right-faced and prepared to march away. Above the spears a tattered moleskin guidon hung limply in the moonlight. Frog sighed, and wondered what the mole's last thoughts had been.

'Useless to look to them for help,' said Manny Rat. 'If you

have any parting words for one another, now is the time to say them.'

'RATIONS!' bellowed the frog. 'FRESH MEAT FOR THE ARMY! RATIONS FOR THE TROOPS! RIGHT HERE!'

'Rations!' came the shrill response across the snow. The compact little mass of black figures grew suddenly large as it wheeled about and sped forward, the spears all pointing in a single direction and the guidon fluttering like hunger's lean banner.

'Stay for dinner, do!' urged Frog as Manny Rat took to his heels, but the thwarted rat made no reply. Running for his life, he vanished in the darkness of the trees as a wave of musk scent surged over the fortune-teller, the father, and the son.

'Uncle Frog!' cried the child. 'The shrews will eat you up!'

'Better they than Manny Rat,' said Frog. Having intended to betray his friends, he had betrayed himself instead, and now, calm and resigned, he waited as the briskly trotting shrews skidded to a halt before him, two or three of the more short-sighted troops bumping into the mouse and his child and knocking them over. All of them were thin and famished-looking, and moved their jaws as if determined to be chewing hard whenever anything should come their way.

'Tough – very hard and tough,' said one, rubbing his nose where he had bruised it on the father's tin.

'Save him for the officer's mess,' said another as he pinched the frog. 'This one's fine. This one's plump and tasty. He smells good.'

'Oh, yes,' said someone else. 'I've had frog. Frog's good.'

A stiff-nosed corporal appeared, looked up at Frog, and took a straw from a mouseskin pouch. 'One frog,' he said, and notched the straw with his teeth; 'two . . . two what?'

'Mice,' said Frog.

'They don't smell like any mice I ever ate,' the corporal said, and bit more notches in his tally. 'Who turned you in anyhow?'

'Destiny,' said Frog.

'You can't trust anybody,' said the corporal. He put away the straw and turned the captives over to a guard. 'All set,' he reported to the sergeant in command of the commissary patrol.

'Let's go then,' said the sergeant. 'And no more fife and drum – we're getting too close to the border.'

'Rations, fall in!' shouted the corporal. The frog and the mouse and his child were hustled to the head of the column. Behind them a little group of captive wood mice shuffled their feet and wept.

'Shut up,' said the guard to the wood mice, 'or I'll stick you with this spear and you'll go bye-bye right now.'

'Forrard, hoo!' yelled the sergeant. The scout with the fox

fire trotted on ahead; the guidon bearer stepped out bravely under the lean banner; the troops shouldered their spears and marched off with short tails whisking, their massed black shadow keeping step with them across the moonlit snow as they herded their rations back to headquarters.

The mouse child, as he walked backwards, found himself facing the drummer boy. 'Is it really a war?' he asked the little soldier.

'Of course it is,' replied the shrew. 'Our territory's all hunted out, so we'll have to fight the shrews down by the stream for theirs.'

'It's the other way around, the way I heard it,' said the fifer. 'I heard *their* territory's all hunted out, and they invaded ours.'

'What's a territory?' asked the mouse child.

'What do you mean, "What's a territory?" ' said the drummer boy. 'A territory's a territory, that's all.'

'Rations don't have territories,' said the fifer.

'Not after we catch them,' said the drummer boy, 'but they do before. *Everybody* does.'

'We didn't,' said the mouse child.

'No wonder you're rations now,' said the little shrew. 'What chance has anybody got without a territory?'

'But what *is* a territory?' asked the mouse child again.

'A territory is your place,' said the drummer boy. 'It's where everything smells right. It's where you know the runways and the hideouts, night or day. It's what you fought for, or what your father fought for, and you feel all safe and strong there. It's the place where, when you fight, you win.'

'That's *your* territory,' said the fifer. 'Somebody else's territory is something else again. That's where you feel all sick and scared and want to run away, and that's where the other side mostly wins.'

The father walked in silence as a wave of shame swept

over him. *What chance has anybody got without a territory!* he repeated to himself and knew the little shrew was right. What chance had they indeed! He saw now that for him and for his son the whole wide world was someone else's territory, on which he could not even walk without someone to wind him up. Frog wound him now as they marched, and the father felt the key turn in his back as a knife turns in a wound.

No one spoke for a time. The wood mice whimpered softly, the shrew's feet pattered on the crusted snow, the frog's matchbox rattled as he hopped, and the tin feet of the mouse and his child scraped steadily ahead to the buzzing of their motor. The whole company were nervously alert as they marched, and the spears clicked against one another, pointing this way and that as the shrews, sniffing incessantly, looked behind them or peered aside into the shadows of the trees along the meadow's edge.

'Where are we now?' said the corporal, his long nose twitching anxiously.

'Almost there, I think,' said the sergeant. The route he was taking was not one that the company had used before, and there was no spoor to guide him or the scout who reconnoitred up ahead; the sergeant was relying on his sense of direction to bring him to an area where he could pick up the scent of his battalion.

'When are we getting back to headquarters?' demanded a shrill voice from the ranks.

'Let's eat now!' yelled someone.

'Knock it off,' snapped the uneasy sergeant, and sniffed the air again.

The frog hopped patiently along without a word. As far as he knew he was hopping to his death, and he was thoroughly disgusted with himself. He had attained his present age, however, by paying closer attention to not being eaten than his enemies could bring to bear on eating him.

Therefore he put aside his fears and opened all his perceptions to every possibility of escape.

Looking down at the tracks made by the mouse and his child as they walked ahead of him, he noticed that the father, owing to one of his legs being bent more than the other, did not walk in a perfectly straight line, but in a series of long arcs that curved always to the left. Being at the head of the column, he had imperceptibly taken the whole company off their course of march, and a sensation of uneasiness had begun to spread through the ranks.

'I feel funny,' said the drummer boy. However soldierly he bore himself, he stood less than two inches high; the moonlit meadow suddenly seemed vast and dangerous around him, and his trembling paws involuntarily rattled a soft tattoo on his drum.

'So do I,' said the fifer, 'And you know why and I know why – we're lost, and we're in *their territory*.' The guidon bearer, the sergeant, and the corporal, as their own misgivings were put into words, stopped short, and the column halted unevenly as each shrew bumped into the one in front of him. The scout, whose sorties had been growing even briefer, snapped back to the company as if connected to them by a rubber band, and hastily buried his fox fire in the snow. The father, unable to push his son past the fifer, trod the snow until his spring ran down.

'Are you scared?' the mouse child asked the drummer boy.

'Me, scared? Never!' declared the young soldier. 'At least I don't *think* I'll be scared. It's my first war, really.' They were in a little hollow screened by a thicket on the windward side. Their voices now were strangely loud in the still air, and everyone fell silent.

'What's going to happen. Uncle Frog?' whispered the mouse child.

'I don't know,' said Frog, 'but look sharp for a chance to escape.'

'War,' muttered the father. 'The dust-bin, the dump, murder, robbery, and war.'

'Shut up,' said the shrew who was guarding them, and drawing in his breath suddenly, fell forward with a spear in his back.

'Ambush!' yelled the sergeant. 'First platoon, move up on the right flank. The rest of you fall back and cover! Fifer, sound Distress!'

The musk scent was overpowering as the shrews re-grouped to face the attack from the thicket, and the little fifer sent the notes of the distress call piping across the moon-lit meadow until a spear cut him short. The drummer boy snatched up the fife, and the piercing call trilled in the moonlight again, drawing another whistling flight of spears. Then the fife was once more silent as the drummer fell with a spear in his throat. He tried to shout, 'Onward, shrews!' but had no breath to say it, and died without a word.

'Here they come!' cried the sergeant, and the enemy shrews were upon them, shrieking their battle cry, 'Ours! Ours! Ours!'

'Now!' said the frog to the father. Keeping low and moving quickly, he pulled three spears from the snow, arming himself with one and placing the others under the father's arms so that they pointed forward over the child's shoulders. He was about to wind the father for their flight when the mouse child's eyes met his. For an instant the frog was held by some silent compulsion while the shrill cry of the battle rose around them; then he knew what the child wanted and dared not ask for. Hesitating only a moment, Frog leaped among the shrews where the fighting was blood-iest, took the nutshell drum from the body of the little soldier, and returning safely, hung it from the mouse child's neck.

'Follow us!' shouted the father to the captives cowering behind them.

'Onward, mice!' cried the child. and felt the little drum resounding to his voice.

The wood mice, with much whimpering, followed, flattening themselves against the snow while spears rattled against father and son and flew over their heads. Frog, ducking and dodging, fought off the shrews that blundered into his path, but both sides were too absorbed in the battle to pursue the fleeing rations.

Once among the trees at the meadow's edge, the surviving wood mice dispersed and ran for their homes, while the breathless frog leaned on his spear and panted, and the mouse and his child strode forward until their spring ran down. Behind them on the snow lay fallen shrews and wood mice, their open mouths still shaping final cries of rage and fear, their open eyes fast glazing in the moonlight. The mouse child stared beyond his father's shoulder at the astonishing stillness of the dead. The father looked at the spears he carried; he had felt the weight of enemies upon them, and for the first time in his life knew what it was to strike a blow for freedom.

'Look!' said Frog. The snow was black with screaming shrews as the opposing armies of meadow and stream, responding to the distress call, converged in the hollow, and the dead and the dying were trampled in alternate waves of attack and retreat.

'Ours! Ours! Ours!' chanted the defenders of their territory, while the attacking shrews, giving ground but always charging again, screamed, 'Onward! Onward! Onward!'

While the frog and the mouse and his child watched from the trees, two weasels came bounding over a rise of ground on the other side of the hollow. Lithe and keen, they seemed almost to slide between the moonbeams as they ran. Then they stopped, their heads swaying snakelike as they sniffed the musk scent.

'I know you'll like this place,' said the female to her mate.

'I came here the other night, and it's really a darling little hollow. There's always something good. Mmm! Smell those shrews!'

'I don't know,' said the male. 'Shrew is what I had for lunch.'

'There's no pleasing you,' said the female. 'And they're such tempting little fellows too.' Below them both armies were dragging off the wounded and the dead; as the moon sank low their moving shadows lengthened on the blood-stained snow; the glittering crust was unbroken by the tiny trampling feet. 'Look,' said the female as both armies drew back and closed ranks for another charge, 'they're all lined up in rows, ever so neat.'

'Oh, all right,' said the male. 'Let's have shrew then. I don't want to argue about it.'

The weasels flowed like hungry shadows down into the hollow, and once among the shrews, struck right and left with lightning swiftness, smiling pleasantly with the blood of both armies dripping from their jaws. Not a single shrew escaped. When the weasels had satisfied their thirst for blood they bounded away, leaving behind them heaps of tiny corpses scattered on the snow.

'This is a *nice* territory,' said the female. 'It's the nicest we've had yet. I'd kind of like to settle down here for a while.'

'It's not bad,' said her mate. 'Not a bad little territory at all. I could see us making a home here.' They nuzzled each other affectionately as they ran, and their heads were so close together that when the horned owl swooped down out of the moonlight his talons pierced both brains at once.

'My land,' wheezed the owl as he rose heavily with the weasels' limp bodies dangling from his claws. 'Two at once! The missus won't believe me when I tell her. Yes-siree!' he chuckled, 'as territories go, this is a mighty good one!'

He flew on, and the earth slid back below him, silver in

the moonlight. Over the Meadow Mutual Hoard and Trust Company he flew, and the fields beyond the woods; over the rubbish-fire beacons of the dump and the windups in the beer-can avenue; over the rats' midway where the carousel played its cracked waltz; over new rubbish hills, and over the charred ruin of a dolls' house with its mansard roof smashed, its lookout missing, its chimneys toppled, its ladies and its gentlemen long gone.

*

The frog and the mouse and his child, seeing no immediate danger after a cautious look all around, left the trees and struck out for the pine woods beyond the stream at the far end of the meadow. The full moon, low behind the black trees, watched them like a yellow eye as they reached the stream and followed it. Frog thumped softly on the snow as he hopped; the matchbox rattled; the clockwork buzzed; the tin feet of the mouse and his child scraped and slid upon the snow; the stream beside them gurgled under the ice.

'Onward, mice!' muttered the father to himself as he pushed his son ahead. Most of the cloth of his trousers had been torn away by spears and his bare tin glinted in the moonlight where his fur was missing. The child, similarly battleworn, listened to the drum that thumped and rattled on his chest, but walked backwards in silence.

'There are the pines on the far side of the stream,' said Frog. 'We can cross here.' He helped the mouse and his child down the bank and on to the ice.

'Destiny has many rivers – ' he began, but never finished the sentence. There was a swoop of soft wings as he spoke, a gust of cold air, and Frog rose up above the stream in the talons of the horned owl's mate. Father and son, knocked flat, heard the fortune-teller's coin clink on the ice beside them. 'Good luck!' called the deep, sad voice of their friend and uncle, and the frog was gone in the last of the moonlight.

*

The sky was brightening into dawn when Manny Rat approached the hollow where the shrews had fought. He moved slowly and laboriously, clanking as he walked, for he had fashioned armour for himself from two tin cans, and thus protected from poisoned spears, had come to snatch his victims from the shrews. The elephant laboured behind him in the snow, her one eye fixed on him as though hatred alone kept her rusty works in motion.

Manny Rat walked through thickets of spear shafts among the silent ranks of the dead, cursing quietly as he looked in vain for signs or remnants of the toy mice and the frog. After making sure that no live shrews lurked nearby, he divested himself of the tin cans, straightened his paisley dressing gown, and considered the situation. 'Well,' he said at length, 'having come this far, I might as well continue. It's really quite remarkable how they keep on going! What a relief it will be to smash them!' Sighing philosophically, he dined on what the weasels had left, then, provisioning the elephant's paper bags for future travel, he took up the trail again.

The sun was up, and the spears in the snow, like gnomons, marked the hour with their shadows, when the bluejay reporter flashed over the battlefield. 'LATE BULLETIN!' he squawked. 'NIGHT BATTLE ON MEADOW BORDER RESULTS IN . . .' He paused and flew lower, in some confusion as to who had won and who had lost. 'VICTORY!' he concluded, and pleased with the sound, extended his headline. 'VICTORY! VICTORY! VICTORY!' he screamed, and was gone into the business of the day.

Behind him on the battlefield two tin cans glinted in the sunlight, and from one of them a scrap of paper fluttered like a little banner in the morning breeze. BONZO Dog Food, said the label, and on it half a little black-and-white spotted dog, wearing a chef's cap, smiled at his image on the smaller BONZO can he carried on his tray.

FOUR

THE mouse and his child lay on the ice where they had fallen, the father's legs moving slowly back and forth as his spring unwound.

'My Uncle Frog is gone!' wept the child. 'What happened?'

'He was taken by an owl, as the weasels were,' the father said. 'He kept his word, and guided us as far as he was able. Now our destined roads have parted, and once more we are alone.' Alone to face Manny Rat, he thought even as he spoke, for he knew that soon or late the rat would be on their trail again. He saw those burning eyes as clearly as if he stood before him now, and heard again the soft voice saying to the fortune-teller, 'Step aside; I'm going to smash your friends.'

The father said nothing more to the child; they lay in silence through the night, while the wind brought them the smell of the pines to remind them of the Christmas tree where they would never dance again.

'Act One, Scene One,' said a scratchy voice across the stream as the sun rose. '*The bottom of a pond: mud, ooze, rubbish, and water plants.*'

'That kills me,' said a second, more resonant voice. 'That is *deep*. That is the profoundest.'

'Shall we call for help?' the mouse child asked his father. 'They don't sound as if they'd hurt us.'

'We'll have to take the chance,' said the father. 'Help!' they both yelled as loudly as they could with their little tin voices. 'Help!'

'*Two tin cans, standing upright, half buried in the mud at centre stage,'* continued the scratchy voice. *'At stage left, a rock.'*

'Help!' called the mouse and his child again.

'A head rises from one of the tin cans,' the voice went on.

'Wait a minute,' said the other voice. 'I heard something. If that's a farmer with a shotgun, get ready to take off fast.'

A large crow came walking out of the pines and cocked his head to listen. A tall, well-set-up bird, he wore his great black, glossy wings in the manner of a cloak thrown carelessly over his shoulders, and he had what his wife and fellow actors admiringly described as 'presence': wherever he was, he simply seemed to be there more intensely than any other bird. 'It's a couple of stranded windups,' he called to his unseen companions.

The crow flew down to where father and son lay on the ice, and there he saw the coin that Frog had dropped. He flipped it up with one foot, caught it in his beak, removed it with a flourish, and held it out at leg's length to look at it. The coin had been gold plated when Frog had found it at the bottom of a pond, but now it was worn down to the original brass. YOU WILL SUCCEED, said the lettering around the rim, and in the centre was a four-leaf clover.

'Well, you've got nothing to worry about,' said Crow to the mouse and his child. 'You will succeed. Says so right here.'

'When?' asked the child.

Crow looked at the other side of the coin, on which a horseshoe appeared, and the partial message YOUR LUCKY DAY IS ... The rest had been obliterated by the hole drilled for the string. 'When your lucky day arrives,' he said, and hung the coin from the mouse child's neck, where it clinked against the drum.

Then he picked up father and son and flew back into the

pines to land beside a rather showy lady crow and three pretty starlings. The other members of the company were a gaunt and dejected-looking rabbit and a brilliantly coloured but frowsy parrot who wore two or three sleeveless dolls' sweaters and a woollen muffler. It was she whose scratchy voice they had heard earlier. Long ago she had been somebody's pet Polly, but having since spread her wings and flown to freedom through an open window, she felt herself entitled to a more resounding name, and now was called Euterpe.

Mrs Crow, who had been stranded more than once herself, was cordial in her welcome. 'After all,' she said, 'they don't eat. They might as well join the company and make themselves useful if they can.' She leaned down to look more closely at the child. 'What do you do when you're wound up?' she asked. 'Do you play that drum?'

'No,' said the child. 'We used to dance.'

'But now we walk,' said the father, 'And behind us an enemy walks faster.'

'That's life,' said Euterpe.

'We're looking for a seal,' the mouse child said.

'And a rat is looking for us,' the father added.

'Two toy mice in search of a seal and followed by a rat! That's too much!' said the starlings together, fluttering up and flapping their wings as they laughed. Crow and Mrs Crow laughed also, while the parrot looked thoughtful.

'She used to have a red and yellow ball on her nose,' said the child. 'We're looking for an elephant too. We're going to have a family.'

'Fantastic!' said the starlings.

'It's got possibilities,' said Crow. He wound up the father and stepped back. 'All right,' he said. 'Let's see what you can do.'

The mouse and his child walked across the snow until they bumped into a twig and fell down. They lay there, the father's legs moving slowly back and forth while the company watched in silence. The sky was bright and cold; the white snow sparkled in the sunlight; a woodpecker drummed beyond the frozen stream, and the wind sighed in the pines. 'Can you help us?' asked the father. 'We must keep moving on; we cannot stop here.'

'Pathos,' said Crow. 'Real pathos.'

'They've definitely got something,' said Mrs Crow, as she helped the mouse and his child to their feet. 'The patter about the seal and the elephant needs working up, but the walk is good and the fall is terrific. Maybe we can use them the next time we do a revue.'

Crow draped a black wing over the shoulders of father

and son. 'Welcome to the Caws of Art Experimental Theatre Group,' he said.

'Last year it was the Caws of Art Classical Repertory Group,' said Mrs Crow.

'You've got to move with the times,' said Crow.

'But we don't want to be in the Caws of Art Experimental Theatre Group,' said the child. 'We've got to find the seal. We were told she was with you. She had a platform on her nose.'

'Who?' said Crow. 'What platform?'

'The seal,' said the child. 'Have you seen a tin seal with a platform on her nose?'

'*That* seal!' said Crow. 'A *windup* seal. Now I remember.' He made a whirling gesture with one wing. 'She did an acrobatic routine with a sparrow?'

'That's right,' said the child.

'Sure,' said Crow. 'That was back when we did the Caws of Art Follies – our best season, as I remember. We had a line of red-hot chickadees in that show that everybody was crazy about.' He shook his head, opened his beak, and shut it with a clack.

'Where did you find her?' asked the child.

'We got her from Manny Rat,' said Crow. 'He books most of the windups. You know him?'

'It is Manny Rat who is following us now, to destroy us,' said the father.

'Oh, it can't be so bad as all that,' said Crow. 'Why in the world would he destroy windups? He fixes them up and sells them. And he's not the rat to destroy his own profits. We paid three bags of jelly beans for that seal, for instance, which is a pretty stiff price for a broken-down windup. I mean, you know, business is business, even if it is show business. They were new jelly beans too – out of a case that fell off the back of a truck.'

'Where is she now?' asked the child.

Crow shrugged. 'Who knows? On tour somewhere, I guess. I traded her to a rabbit with a travelling flea circus.'

'For what?' asked the child.

'For a pair of doll's roller skates and·part of a gyroscope,' said Crow. 'Let's go, everybody! I want to run through *Dog* again, from the top.'

'Won't you help us?' begged the father.

'Look,' said Crow, 'give yourself a chance to calm down a little, and we'll talk about it later. Believe me, you're safe here. Nobody's going to bother you while you're with me.' He struck a boxing pose, grimaced ferociously, and launching a slow-motion roundhouse blow, gently nudged the father's jaw with one wing. Then he winked at him and turned to the company. 'All right,' he said, 'let's get started.'

'Are you absolutely sure you want to do *The Last Visible Dog* tonight?' said Mrs Crow.

'Sure, I'm sure,' said Crow. 'It's the hottest thing we've got. It's new. It's far out. It's a play with a message.'

'What's the message?' said Mrs Crow.

'I don't know,' said Crow. 'But I know it's there, and that's what counts.'

'It seems to me *The Woodchuck's Revenge* is a better bet,' said Euterpe, who was, if not the company's lyric muse, at any rate their repertory, since it was she who stored in her memory all the plays presented by them. 'You can't go wrong with a plot like *Woodchuck*,' she asserted. 'The whole family loses its territory when the fox forecloses the mortgage and throws them out of their den.'

'Territory again,' said the father to the child. 'Must I always be remined of our placelessness!'

'If we could find the dolls' house, that could be our territory,' said the child. 'Couldn't it, Papa?' He felt the weight of the coin on the string around his neck. 'Maybe we'll succeed,' he said. 'Maybe we'll have a lucky day.'

66

Euterpe, meanwhile, was still putting forward the merits of *The Woodchuck's Revenge*. '*Banker Foxcraft!*' she declaimed. '*More deadly in his treachery than trapper who with sharp-toothed steel besets the woodland path. What new pitfall has his perfidy prepared for us!* That's always been sure-fire,' she said.

'Look, Euterpe,' said Crow, 'as Director of the Caws of Art, I intend to further the cause of Art. We'll do *Dog* tonight. All right – Act One, Scene One. Let's go.'

'*The bottom of a pond,*' squawked Euterpe: '*mud, ooze, rubbish, and water plants. Two tin cans, standing upright, half buried in the mud at centre stage. At stage left, a rock. A head rises from one of the tin cans. It is the head of Furza. The head of Wurza rises from the other tin can. Gretch enters stage right and crosses to the rock.*'

'Some play,' said the rabbit who was Gretch. 'I don't get any lines until the third act. All I do is stand on that rock.'

Crow silenced the rabbit with a look, and turned to Mrs Crow. 'All right,' he said, 'Furza speaks first. That's you.'

'What's the latest?' said Mrs Crow, as Furza.

'Latest what?' replied Crow, as Wurza.

'Ooze news,' said Furza.

'Dogs,' said Wurza. 'A manyness of dogs. A moreness of dogs. A too-muchness of dogs. Also a jiggling and a wiggling.'

'A jiggling and a wiggling of what?'

'Of nothing.'

'Where, O, where was it, for goodness' sake?'

'Out among the out among the out among the dots.'

After which Crow stepped out of his role and said, 'You feel it building?'

'No,' said Mrs Crow. 'I'll be honest with you. I don't feel it building.'

'Never mind,' said Crow. 'Just let it happen. Your line.'

'Where among the dots?' said Mrs Crow.

'Out among the dots beyond . . .'

'Yes, yes. Go on. Beyond?'

'Beyond the . . .'

'Don't stop now . . . Beyond the . . .?'

'BEYOND THE LAST VISIBLE DOG!' shouted Crow. 'There!' he said to his wife. 'See how it pays off? Up and up and up, and then Zonk! BEYOND THE LAST VISIBLE DOG!'

'It's getting me now,' said Mrs Crow. 'But what does it mean?'

Crow flung wide his broad wings like a black cloak. 'What *doesn't* it mean!' he said. 'There's no end it – it just goes on and on until it means anything and everything, depending on who you are and what your last visible dog is.'

' "Beyond the last visible dog," ' said the mouse child to his father. 'Where is that, I wonder?'

'I don't know,' said the father, 'but those words touch something in me – something half remembered, half forgotten – that escapes me just as it seems almost clear.'

'Do you think that's where the rabbit and the flea are?' said the child. 'Shall we find the seal and the elephant and the dolls' house out among the dots?'

'We can't find anything unless we continue to move ahead,' said the father, 'and I don't suppose there's any chance of that until after the performance.'

The rehearsal continued through the afternoon, while the starlings set up scenery and props on the open ground beyond the pine woods, where a bowl-shaped hollow formed a natural amphitheatre. Towards sunset the bluejay was heard, screaming, 'CAWS OF ART PRESENTS – What are you presenting?' he yelled as he flew overhead.

'We'll announce it at curtain time,' said Crow. 'I want the audience to come to it with an open mind.'

'PRESENTS EXCITING NEW PLAY,' shouted the

jay. 'BANK-ROBBER WINDUPS MAKE DRA-
MATIC BOW TONIGHT.' And he was gone before the
crow could correct him.

'That's pretty fancy billing for a couple of unknowns,'
said Crow. Bird of the world that he was, he refrained from
questioning his new recruits about their past.

'We have a small following,' said the father wryly, and in
his mind's eye he saw Manny Rat.

When evening came the full moon, rising honey-coloured
above the pines, showed a scattered crowd converging in the
snowy bowl. The animals and birds paid their acorns,
beechnuts, seeds, and grubs, along with turnips and dead
beetles saved for the occasion, and were ushered by the
starlings to their places, where they combined sniffs, growls,
whines, and twitters in the general murmur of an audience
waiting for an entertainment to begin.

The crowd filled up a semicircle of the slope in tiers,
facing the flat open space that was the stage at the centre of
the hollow. There were pines at both sides and on the slope
at the rear of the stage, and a tattered length of brocaded
crimson velvet, attached to two of the trees, was the curtain.
From behind it the mouse and his child and the little troupe
peeped out at the audience.

'That's a good house,' said Crow as the bowl filled up.
'There *is* a place for Art in our meadows. There is a genuine
need.'

'There's a need for something,' said Mrs Crow. 'Let's hope
it's for *The Last Visible Dog*.'

Now the starlings rushed back from their ticket-taking
and ushering duties to sing an overture, and the lively music
lilted over the moonlit meadow. The audience sighed and
leaned back, and Crow strode onstage in front of the curtain, throwing back his wings to receive a burst of applause.

'Thank you,' said Crow, 'thank you. As you know, the

Caws of Art have stood for the best in wholesome family entertainment for longer than most of us care to remember. We have brought you classics and chorus girls, always moving with the times and always striving to offer art that is new and vital.' He paused, and his voice took on a more serious note. 'Tonight,' he said, 'we continue that tradition. We offer you the newest effort of one of the deepest thinkers of our time. The Caws of Art Experimental Theatre Group proudly presents *The Last Visible Dog*, a tragi-comedy in three acts by C. Serpentina.'

There were scattered groans amidst the applause that followed. A possum shifted uneasily in his seat and said to his wife, 'I'm afraid he means business this time.'

'Stay awake, that's all,' said the lady as the starlings lifted the curtain to reveal two large rusty grapefruit-juice cans in which sat Crow and Mrs Crow, their heads covered by their black wings. Euterpe's voice was heard offstage, setting the scene. '*The bottom of a pond*,' she squawked: '*mud, ooze, rubbish, and water plants. Two tin cans, standing upright, half buried in the mud at centre stage*.'

An irate weasel rose from the audience, baring his white teeth in a snarl. 'You watch that stuff!' he shouted. 'We don't want none of your modern filth around here!'

'Tell 'em, Alf!' called one of his friends, and a low growl ran through the crowd.

Crow and Mrs Crow duly rose from their tin cans as Wurza and Furza. The rabbit, as Gretch, entered and stood on his stone, shading his eyes with one paw as he looked around, hopeful of investing his silence with heavy meaning before he settled into immobility.

'Get that phony rabbit out of here!' yelled a tired porcupine. 'Bring on the chickadees!' His fellow playgoers broke out in laughter and catcalls, and the actors did not become audible until Wurza reached the line 'A manyness of dogs. A moreness of dogs. A too-muchness of dogs.'

'That's what this play is,' shouted an enraged marten. 'Too much of a dog!'

'The meadow isn't ready for this yet,' said the local field-mouse critic to his wife.

'And neither are the woods,' said she.

'Also a jiggling and a wiggling,' continued Wurza, scanning the crowd nervously.

'A jiggling and a wiggling of what?' said Furza.

'Of nothing.'

'That does it!' yelled Alf the weasel. 'Let's go, boys!'

'Look out!' screamed Mrs Field-Mouse Critic, but she screamed too late. The starlings backstage fluttered up in time to escape, but Crow and Mrs Crow disappeared in a rush of weasels before they could get off the ground, and the rabbit lay dead, his lifeblood staining the moonlit snow around him.

'One seldom gets anything really *complete* from these road companies,' said the field-mouse critic.

Mrs Crow, scattering weasels right and left with her wings, cried, 'Hoodlums! You don't deserve Art!'

Crow defended his wife and himself like the veteran trouper he was, but they were unable to break clear. 'Come on, fellows,' he gasped, 'you're acting like a bunch of hay-seeds!'

The mouse and his child, unwound and motionless, watched the disaster, while Euterpe, on a bough above them, swore softly to herself. 'This looks like the end of the Caws of Art,' she said. 'In a couple of minutes there'll be nothing left but fur and feathers and a few bones.'

'Can't you do something?' said the child.

'What would you suggest?' asked the parrot.

'Wind us up,' said the father, 'and send us onstage.'

'Certainly,' said the flabbergasted Euterpe. 'Why not!' She wound up the father, and shaking her head, watched him walk across the snow, pushing the child before him.

The weasels who were striving ardently to end the Crows' career looked up as the backward-walking mouse child bumped into them and stopped, the father continuing to tread the snow without being able to move forward.

'Excuse me,' said the child.

'What is it?' said Alf.

Row by row the crowd on the slope stood up for a better view of the two small figures, and some of the playgoers began to titter.

'We were wondering, sir, whether you might have seen a seal?' said the child.

'A seal?' said the weasel.

'That's right,' said the father. 'We're looking for a seal – and there's a rat looking for us.' Crow and Mrs Crow listened as they lay on their backs, wings folded prayerfully, while several grinning weasels sat on them.

'She's probably out beyond the last visible dog by now,' said the child.

'And he's probably hiding behind the last visible pine,' said the father.

'She used to have a red and yellow ball on her nose,' said the child.

'But she doesn't have a ball any more,' said the father, and there was more laughter from the crowd, this time louder than before. Crow and Mrs Crow let out their breath in one joint sigh.

'Go on, Alf! Help them find the seal!' called the weasel's friends.

'Or at least stand aside and let us go on before our spring runs down,' said the father.

'We've got to find an elephant too,' said the child; 'then

we're going to look for a territory of our own,' and the crowd roared its approval.

'That little act has something,' said the field-mouse critic to his wife. 'I think that *Last Visible Dog* business was just the buildup for this. The whole thing was a joke. Too bad it backfired on the rabbit.' Animals sitting near the critic heard, and passed the word along. 'They're marvellous!' said a mole. 'They're almost animal-like!'

The weasels onstage chuckled good-naturedly while father and son walked straight ahead until they bumped into the rabbit's rock and fell over. The crowd laughed until it cried.

'Do it again!' shouted the audience. 'Encore!'

The weasels cleared the stage, the crows flew up into the pines, and father and son were carried back to where they had made their entrance.

As the mouse father, rewound by a helpful weasel, started once more across the stage, he looked beyond his son and saw a familiar figure waiting in the shadows of the pines with a heavy rock uplifted. The child, walking backwards, heard his father whisper, 'Manny Rat!'

'Help!' the mouse child cried. But Manny Rat was downwind; no one else had seen or scented him as yet. The audience laughed, anticipating new comic variations in the toy-mouse act. The irony was too much for the child; it made him giddy. 'Just let it happen,' he said to his father. 'Your line.'

'Banker Ratsneak!' yelled the father, *'more deadly in his treachery than trapper who with sharp-toothed steel besets the woodland path!'*

Manny Rat, watching the two small figures advancing towards him in the moonlight, was startled and made vastly ill at ease by the father's shout. He wondered whether it might not be wise to withdraw for the moment, and he turned to go back through the pines to where he had left the elephant. But the audience had moved in close around the stage; he could not escape unnoticed.

'*Banker Ratsneak!*' yelled the mouse child at the top of his tin voice. '*What new pitfall has his perfidy prepared for us!*'

'Ah!' said the audience, and settled back to watch contentedly.

'Does he hound us still?' declaimed the father, ' – he who drove us forth to wander denless through the world?'

'He hounds us still!' the child replied, still advancing backwards towards Manny Rat, who could retreat no farther, and now tried to make himself as small as possible.

'Banker Ratsneak, skulking in the shadows!' called the father. 'Come out and face your victims! The day of reckoning has come – this final, fateful day that settles all accounts, this day that shall leave one of us to share a territory with the worms!'

'Come out!' the audience roared as one. 'Banker Ratsneak, come out!'

'What kind of an outfit is this?' complained Alf the weasel. 'When they finally give us something we can get our teeth into, the actors fall asleep on their cues!' He strode across the stage into the wings, growled, 'Let's get on with it!' and pulled out Manny Rat.

'Unhand me!' cried the rat, and improvising desperately, he crept onstage. 'I, Banker Ratsneak, have come here to collect a debt long overdue!' he wailed. 'I will have justice!'

'Villain!' screamed the crowd. 'Territory stealer!'

'Tremendous talent, that rat,' said the field-mouse critic to his wife. 'How well he plays the villain! I've never seen a character I detested more thoroughly!' The rest of the spectators, all of whom shared, uncritically, the same emotion, hissed and booed the hapless rat.

Manny Rat, who would have been well content to abandon

74

his role, could scarcely make himself heard. 'Justice!' He wept, and the audience, responding eagerly, rushed the stage and mobbed him.

'I always gave Manny Rat credit for more sense than that,' said Crow to Mrs Crow. 'What in the world made him want to break into show business?'

'Everybody gets the bug at one time or another,' said Mrs Crow, shouting above the uproar on the stage.

'Help!' screamed Manny Rat, rising to the surface of the crowd like foam upon an angry ocean.

'Sorry,' said Crow, as the crowd rolled over the rat again. 'Once you go onstage, you'll have to take your chances like the rest of us.'

Bitten, clawed, and pinched by bird and beast, Manny Rat fought like a demon, while the mouse and his child, having for the moment escaped demolishment by him, were in immediate danger of being trampled flat by the enthusiasts who stormed the stage.

'Onward!' said the child wildly to no one in particular.

'And upward,' replied his father as they felt themselves lifted into the air. Euterpe, the repertory parrot, seeing their plight, had sailed into the tumult in a blur of bright feathers and frayed sweaters, and now winged up into the night carrying the mouse and his child in her claws.

Circling over the pines, the parrot looked down and assessed the situation. The entire Caws of Art company, with the exception of the luckless rabbit, were safe – at least until their next performance. The mass of struggling figures onstage separated, and Manny Rat streaked off across the snow with several of the more diligent weasels in hot pursuit, while the rest of the audience abandoned themselves to general riot and thereby purged themselves of all remaining pity and terror.

'That's show business,' said Euterpe, 'and I've had enough of it for a while. How about you?'

'I think we have sufficiently furthered the Caws of Art,' said the father, 'and I have no intention of continuing a theatrical career.'

'Where are you bound for now?' asked Euterpe. 'I don't want to fly in circles all night.'

'We don't know,' said the father.

'Let it be south, then,' said the parrot, 'because that's where I'm heading. I can use a vacation.' She flew higher, set a straight course, and the pine woods and the Caws of Art were left behind.

*

The parrot's wings fanned gusts of cold air on the mouse and his child, and the darkness flowed by on either side. The moon had set; below them all was dim and grey. The father and son felt the wind race like a road unwinding underneath their feet as, motionless, they travelled on.

'I wonder what happened to Manny Rat,' said the child. 'I wonder if he got away.'

'If he did, we can expect to see him again,' said the father. 'He seems determined to smash us, and I don't think he'll give up.'

'Neither will we,' said the child. 'Will we, Papa?'

The father said nothing, and the child's only answer was the wind that whistled by them as they flew.

'We'll find the elephant and the seal, and we'll find the dolls' house too, and have our own territory, won't we, Papa?'

'You simply won't understand how it is,' said the father. 'How can we find anything? How can we ever hope to have our own territory?'

'But look how far we've come!' said the child. 'And think of all we've done! We got out of the dump; we came through the war safely; we saved the Caws of Art.'

'We escaped after the attempted bank robbery and survived the war only because we had Frog to help us,' said the father. 'And we saved the Caws of Art by making animals laugh at us. They laughed because we have no teeth or claws and can do nothing for ourselves. They laughed because we are ridiculous.' Then he was silent, looking down at the child who hung from his arms in the darkness, the nutshell drum and good-luck coin swinging from his neck.

'Believe me,' said Euterpe, 'Crow doesn't think you're ridiculous, and neither do I. What you did was pretty clever, and it was brave too. You might have been smashed by that mob.'

'Yes,' said the father, 'we're brave and clever – but not clever enough to wind ourselves up, unfortunately. If only we could!'

'Ah!' said Euterpe. 'There's nothing you can do about that. Although, come to think of it, maybe there is.'

'What do you mean?' asked the father.

'The beaver pond isn't far out of my way,' said Euterpe. 'Old Muskrat lives there. Ever heard of him?'

'No,' said the father.

'Well,' said Euterpe, 'except for Manny Rat, he's the only one I know who can do anything with clockwork. He figures out all kinds of things.' She changed course and swung north. 'He's fixed broken windups for the Caws of Art once or twice,' she said, 'so maybe he can help you too.'

'We're not broken,' said the father. 'Not yet.'

'I mean, maybe he can fix you so you can wind yourselves up,' said Euterpe. 'I've heard he can do almost anything.'

The parrot flew steadily on, and the child, hanging from his father's hands, now saw again the bright star Sirius. It seemed to fly onwards, keeping pace beside them through the distant sky. As before, the child found its light a comfort. His good-luck coin clinked against his drum, and now he felt luckier than ever before. 'Maybe we shan't always be helpless, Papa,' he said. 'Maybe we'll be self-winding some day.'

'Maybe,' said his father.

Below them, scattered houses and farms gave way to wooded hills, and the parrot flew lower. The trees came close as Euterpe swooped down to glide over a valley where a stream widened into a frozen pond. At one end of the pond was an irregular dam made of saplings and cut branches, and below the dam the ice-covered stream continued through the valley.

'That's the beaver dam,' said the parrot as they flew over it, 'and that big snowy mound in the middle of the pond is the beaver lodge. Muskrat has a smaller one right over there, and the entrance tunnel is somewhere on the bank. I think I see his tracks.' She landed at the edge of the pond and set down the mouse and his child on the ice.

'Muskrat'll be sure to find you here,' she said, 'and if anybody can do anything for you, he can.' Father and son felt a wingtip brush them softly as Euterpe took off. 'Good-bye and good luck,' she said, and was gone.

FIVE

THE mouse and his child stood in the darkness and heard the wind whistling over the ice and snow. Under the wind the winter silence waited, and the ice creaked with the cold. Hours passed, and the sky was growing light when the child, who stood facing the bank, said, 'Someone's coming.'

'Is it Muskrat?' asked the father.

'I don't know,' said the child. 'He doesn't look anything like Manny Rat. He's larger and stouter. He has a different kind of tail. And he has a nice face and he limps.'

The muskrat, who looked somewhat like a large brown meadow mouse, approached them slowly. He had lost one leg in a trap, and as he walked he bobbed with a step, step, hop – step, step, hop. His whole manner suggested one continuous train of solid, round, furry thought, and he was mumbling softly to himself.

Muskrat looked up as he bumped into the mouse and his child. 'You're a little early,' he said, 'but that's all right. We can start right here. The lesson for today is the Them Tables. Begin.' He settled back on his haunches and waited.

'I don't know what you mean,' said the mouse father.

'Very well,' said Muskrat, 'I'll help you. Them times Us equals?'

'I don't know,' said the father. 'Really, I – '

'Equals *Bad*,' said Muskrat, whacking the ice with the flat of his tail. 'You were supposed to have learned that.'

'I'm sorry,' said the mouse father.

'Don't be sorry,' said Muskrat. 'Come next time with your lesson prepared. Continue, please. Them plus Trap times Us equals?'

'Worse?' said the mouse child.

'Good boy!' said Muskrat. He came closer and peered nearsightedly at father and son. 'I beg your pardon,' he said. 'I took you for two of my regular pupils. You're new here, then?' He wrinkled his nose. 'You smell a little Themmy. Been in a trap, have you? You must tell me about it. Come over to my place and visit for a while.'

'You'll have to wind me up,' said the father. 'There's a key in the middle of my back.'

Muskrat looked at the key. 'Of course,' he said as he wound it, 'I remember now: Key times Winding equals Go. She had just such a key in her back.'

'Who?' said the father.

'The tin seal,' said Muskrat.

'The seal!' said the child. 'Did she have a platform on her nose?'

'No,' said Muskrat. 'There was only a metal rod that turned, and that was how she used to wind up string for me. Many a cosy evening we spent that way. Charming young lady!' He smiled, lapsing into a silent reverie.

'Where had she come from?' asked the child.

'Who?' said Muskrat.

'The seal.'

'Ah, the seal! She had been travelling with a rabbit flea circus, but the whole concern broke up not far from here. A fox ate the rabbit, the fleas joined the fox, and the seal came to stay with me.'

'Where is she now?' asked the father as they walked towards the other side of the pond.

'I don't know,' said Muskrat. 'She found the life here dull after a time, and went off with a kingfisher. Was she a friend of yours?'

'We were close,' said the father, 'long ago.'

'Well, that's how it is,' said Muskrat. He shook his head thoughtfully as he went with his step, step, hop – step, step, hop. 'Why into Here often equals There, and so one moves about.'

'You have a strange way of speaking,' said the mouse father.

'I'm always looking for the Hows and the Whys and the Whats,' said Muskrat. 'That is why I speak as I do. You've heard of Muskrat's Much-in-Little, of course?'

'No,' said the child. 'What is it?'

Muskrat stopped, cleared his throat, ruffled his fur, drew himself up, and said in ringing tones, 'Why times How equals What.' He paused to let the words take effect. 'That's Muskrat's Much-in-Little,' he said. He ruffled his fur again and slapped the ice with his tail. 'Why times How equals What,' he repeated. 'Strikes you all of a heap the first time you hear it, doesn't it? Pretty well covers everything! I'm a little surprised that you haven't heard of it before, I must say. It caused a good deal of comment both over and under the pond, and almost everyone agreed that the ripples from it were ever-widening.'

'Your work is, of course, known everywhere,' said the mouse father, 'and although we were not acquainted with Muskrat's Much-in-Little we have heard a great deal about you.'

'Ah!' said Muskrat. He smiled a little smile and groomed his fur complacently. 'Yes,' he said. 'I have some small reputation, perhaps. I am not entirely unknown. Not that I care about such things.' He wound up the father again, and they continued across the ice.

'We have travelled far to see you,' said the father, 'in the hope of learning how to be – '

'Like me,' said Muskrat. 'I thank you humbly for the compliment, and I have the most profound respect for your admiration. Yes. There is a small but growing circle of students and followers whom I hope to guide along the path to – '

'Self-winding,' said the father.

'I beg your pardon,' said Muskrat. 'What did you say?'

'Self-winding,' said the child. 'We want to be self-winding, so we can wind ourselves up. Euterpe the parrot said that you've fixed broken windups. Can't you fix us?'

'I'm afraid that's a little out of my line,' said Muskrat. 'Oh, I've tinkered with clockwork now and then, but I have long since gone beyond the limits of mere mechanical invention. That's applied thought, you see, and my real work is in the realm of pure thought. There is nothing quite like the purity of pure thought. It's the cleanest work there is, you might say.' He nodded and mumbled softly to himself as he bobbed along with his uneven limping gait.

The sun was up when they reached the beaver lodge, and the snowy dome gleamed rosy in the morning light. Muskrat sniffed as he looked up at the structure that towered above them, its snow-covered smoothness broken by projecting brush and twigs and the cut ends of saplings. 'They came here a few seasons back,' he said, 'when there was nothing here but a little trickle through the grass. They built the dam, made the pond, put up this lodge, and they pretty well run the whole place now.'

There was a murmur of voices inside the lodge, and Muskrat leaned close to listen. 'Always the same thing,' he said. 'How many aspens they've cut down. How many birches. How they're going to improve the dam next year. Dull fellows! Yet I suppose they have their place. It is, after all, their pond that supports my pure thought. And in spite of the hurly-burly of industry and the working-class atmosphere, my roots are here. Not only my roots, but my stalks and leaves – arrowhead and smartweed, cattails and wild rice. Yes,' he said, 'this is my home, where my work has brought me pondwide respect and esteem. Let the beavers have their wealth! I am content with the treasures of the mind.' He smiled with satisfaction, and limped along beside the mouse and his child with a step, step, hop – step, step, hop.

'Here's my place,' said Muskrat, as they came to the smaller of the two domes on the ice. 'But we can't get into it here; the entrance is underwater, from a tunnel on the far bank.' From inside the lodge came the sound of two young muskrats laughing. 'Merry little rascals!' said Muskrat. 'That must be Jeb and Zeb, come for their lesson.'

'Hee!' said one of the voices inside the lodge. 'Hee times Hoo equals Heehoo!'

'Rinkum times Dinkum equals Rinkumdinkumdoo!' said the other.

'What are they talking about?' asked the mouse child.

'They're making fun of my much-in-little,' said Muskrat, managing a smile. 'High-spirited lads!'

'Jeb,' said the voice of Zeb, 'what do you want to be when you grow up?'

'A beaver,' replied Jeb without hesitation.

'A beaver?' said Zeb.

'A beaver!' echoed Muskrat.

'Right!' said Jeb, clicking his teeth and whacking the floor of the lodge as hard as he could with the flat of his tail. 'Beavers *do* things! They cut down trees! CHONK! BONK! Make dams! SPLASH! KERPLONK! Beavers get rich!'

'Maybe old Muskrat knows all that stuff too,' said Zeb. 'Maybe he could cut down trees if he wanted to.'

'Who, him?' snorted Jeb. 'He can't do anything! My daddy says old Muskrat got caught in a trap once and it shook his brains up. All he's good for now is teaching kids the Them Tables.'

'*Ahem!*' said Muskrat. He climbed on to the lodge and jumped up and down several times, stamping heavily on the roof. There was instant silence inside. '*Boys!*' he called.

'Yes, sir!' came the polite response.

'No lesson today,' said Muskrat. 'Very busy. Great many things to do. Come back next week. Bye-bye.'

There was a single splash inside the lodge as Jeb and Zeb dived into the water and swam home under the ice.

'You were saying – ' began the father, hoping to bring the muskrat back to the subject of self-winding.

Muskrat turned away from him. 'Crushed!' he said in a choked voice. 'I am utterly and completely crushed! Good for nothing but to teach children the Them Tables! *That's* what the whole pond thinks of me!' he whispered brokenly. '*That's* the sort of respect they've had for me!'

'You mustn't be so upset,' said the father. 'Your work is admired everywhere. That is why we came to you for – '

'Beavers!' hissed Muskrat, doing a little limping dance of irritation. Then he began to pace back and forth slowly: step, step, hop – step, step, hop. 'CHONK! BONK!' he said. 'Beavers *do* things, eh? Very well, then, I'll do something!'

'What will you do?' asked the mouse child.

'I don't know,' said Muskrat, 'but it'll be something that'll make them sit up and take notice!' His pacing quickened to a stepstep hoppity – stepstep hoppity. Then he stopped.

'I can't pace right any more,' he said. 'My best Much-in-Little thinking was done before I lost my leg in the trap; I can't reason as I did when I was whole. There's a universal rhythm that the mind must catch. I used to feel it; now I don't. My mental powers are hobbled, like my gait.'

'Perhaps,' said the mouse father, lurching ahead on his bent legs, 'if we pace for you until you solve your problem, you might help us with ours?'

'What's that?' asked Muskrat.

'What's what?' said the father.

'The problem you want help with,' said Muskrat.

'SELF-WINDING!' said the father.

'No need to shout,' said Muskrat. 'Yes, that seems fair

enough, and your pacing, while lacking something in style, is nonetheless steady. Let's go to my workroom and get started.'

They had reached the shore of the pond, and Muskrat took the mouse and his child down into the tunnel that led to his underground den. Crystals of frost winked from the frozen walls, and the dark, cold, chthonic smell of earth pervaded the slanting passage. A faint, greenish glow appeared ahead at the doorway of the den.

'This is where I do most of my thinking,' said Muskrat. 'The lodge in the pond is rather too much in the middle of things.' He followed the mouse and his child into the room. A little group of firefly students had lit up when the musk-rat's familiar step was heard in the tunnel, and now they said in unison, 'Good morning, sir.' Devoted followers who had outstayed the summer, they lived in a glass jar in a corner, and their dormitory cast its pale and blinking glow on the clutter all around them. An oilcan and a ball of string lay among mussel shells and the forgotten nibbled ends of roots and stalks beside a small terrestrial pencil-sharpener globe; a BONZO Dog Food can stood filled with salvage from the bottom of the pond: rusty beer-can openers, hairpins, fishhooks, corroded cotter pins, tangles of wire, drowned flash-light batteries, a jackknife with a broken blade, and part of a folding ruler. Near it sprawled improvisations of dis-coloured pipe cleaners, tobacco tins, old fishing-licence badges, draggled wet- and dry-fly feathers, coils of catgut, jointed lures that bristled with hooks and staring eyes – all the neglected apparatus of past experiments in applied thought. Against the wall leaned a bit of broken slate with X's, Y's, and Z's scrawled on it. The air was still and warm, the odour studious and strong.

Muskrat rubbed his paws together, hummed a little tune, heaved everything anyhow into the centre of the den, and smoothed a circular track around the floor. 'Now, then,' he said, and winding up the father, he started the mouse and his child on their rounds.

The curved walls of the den kept them in the track. The child's good-luck coin gleamed in the pale light of the fireflies as it clinked against the drum; the glass-bead eyes of father and son caught the glow as — now seen, now lost behind the jumble — they circled steadily around the muskrat while he pondered.

'We're going in a circle again, Papa,' said the child, 'but this time it's going to get us somewhere.'

'Yes,' said the father, 'things seem to be looking up. And Manny Rat will certainly have lost our trail by now; I'm beginning to think Frog may have been wrong about the enemy waiting for us at the end.'

'And maybe Uncle Frog wasn't killed by the horned owl,' said the child. 'Maybe he'll find us again. He's very wise.'

'Wise or not, I don't think anyone returns from the horned owl's talons,' said the father sadly.

'I beg your pardon,' said Muskrat, 'but I must ask you to

be quiet. Absolute silence is essential to much-in-little thinking.' The mouse and his child said no more, but paced in silence.

'First,' said Muskrat, 'we must define the problem; that's how you begin.'

'Hear him!' said the senior fireflies, and the junior ones made mental notes. Muskrat sat on his haunches, rocking slightly, his whiskers quivering with the intensity of his thought, which he interrupted only when it was necessary to wind up the mouse father.

'The problem,' he said, 'is to do something, something big, something resultful – something, in short, that will make both a crash and a splash and show the whole pond how truly much is meant by Muskrat's Much-in-Little.'

'Why times How equals What!' blurted one of the smaller fireflies, on the chance that an oral examination was taking place.

'Quiet!' said his elders, and quenched his light.

'Now,' continued Muskrat, 'what's big and crashful and splashful? CHONK! BONK! The felling of a tree. Suppose we say, then, that the problem is to fell a tree.' His usually mild eye flashed with something more than the fireflies' feeble light. 'A big tree,' he said.

'To fell a tree,' repeated the mouse father as he paced.

'Hush!' said Muskrat. 'Now, who fells trees? Beavers. How do beavers fell trees?' He clicked his teeth.

'Teeth!' said the mouse child.

'*Do* be quiet,' said Muskrat. 'Teeth is right. The teeth of beavers are of the proper size, shape, and sharpness for cutting down trees. Mine are not, but theirs are. When a beaver gnaws at a tree for a period of time, that tree will fall.' He picked up a withered brown arrowhead stalk and chewed it reflectively. 'So we may now reduce this data to the following much-in-little – '

'Pay attention!' said the senior fireflies, glowing brighter.

'Beaver plus Teeth times Gnaw times Time times Tree equals Treefall,' said Muskrat.

'Bravo!' the mouse father cried out involuntarily.

'Thank you,' said Muskrat. 'That's first-rate pacing, by the way.' He drew himself up and launched himself anew upon his thoughts. 'Let us now disassociate the tooth from the beaver,' he said.

'How his mind soars!' exclaimed the fireflies all together, and intensified their light, so that the glass eyes of the fish lures blazed up in the gloom, staring in wild surmise.

'You've got to be able to make those daring leaps or you're nowhere,' said Muskrat. 'Where was I?'

'Disassociate the tooth from the beaver,' said the mouse father.

'Yes,' said Muskrat, 'and consider it simply as *any* tooth of the proper kind, or as we might say, Tooth^K.'

'Tooth^K,' said the mouse child.

'Tooth^K times Gnaw,' said the father.

'Tooth^K times Gnaw times Time times Tree equals Treefall,' said Muskrat. 'Wait – it's coming to me now!' The fireflies had dimmed a little; now they kindled up again. 'I've got it!' shouted Muskrat.

'What?' said the mouse and his child together.

'X!' said Muskrat, 'X!'

The fireflies abandoned all reserve, and flashed with such a light that Muskrat's shadow loomed up huge and black upon the wall behind him.

'He's done it!' said the father to the child. 'He's made the leap.'

'X!' said Muskrat, dancing about with a steppity hop, and bumping into things with every step. 'It needn't be a tooth at all! Anything of the proper *k*, which is to say size, shape, and sharpness, will do it.' He limped to the broken piece of slate, hastily rubbed it clean with his paw, wrote $XT = T^F$, and sat back, rocking on his haunches. 'X times Tree equals

Treefall,' he said huskily, and crooned beneath his breath a little song of triumph.

'Ah!' said the fireflies. They blazed up once more all together, then sank back, exhausted, to a pale glimmer. The room grew dim and dark.

'Tremendous!' said the mouse father. 'Simply tremendous.'

'Well, we've solved the problem,' said Muskrat, 'and I tell you frankly I couldn't have done it without you. Steady pacing is what does the trick.'

'Thank you,' said the mouse father. 'Now we can go on to the problem of self-winding.'

'Yes, indeed,' said Muskrat, ' – as soon as we've felled the tree. There's very little to it, I'm sure, once you've got the X, and I'm off to find one now.'

'What will the X be?' asked the mouse child.

'I don't know,' said Muskrat, 'but I'll know it when I see it.' And he was out of the den, into the tunnel, and gone, with a step, step, hop – step, step, hop.

*

The muskrat was away for several days. The fireflies, out of courtesy, kept going at half strength the whole time, while the mouse and his child, unwound, stared at the much-in-little on the dim slate and smelled the darkness of the earth.

When they heard the muskrat's footsteps in the tunnel on the day of his return, the sound was new and different: scuff, scuff, slide, hop – scuff, scuff, slide, hop. At length Muskrat came into the den and flung down an axe, the handle of which had been broken off short.

'Here it is,' he said. 'X. I found it at a *Them* place, and I must say I don't care for the smell of it, besides which it's a great deal bigger than I'd like it to be.' He limped around the axe, looking down at it uneasily. 'Well, why not?' he said.

'Once you accept X, the size doesn't really matter. Now, then – to work! Our objective is ... ah ... our goal is ... um ...'

'To fell a tree,' said the mouse father.

'Exactly,' said Muskrat. 'You have a head for detail; I admire that. Now to begin! For applied thought you need string,' he said. After finding his ball of string where it lay in the clutter, he took the axe and the mouse and his child out through the tunnel and up to the stand of birch and aspen trees beside the pond, where the beavers had been working earlier that year. Gnawed and pointed stumps stood everywhere, casting their lopped-off shadows on the snow among the full-length shadows of the bare trees all around them. Muskrat's breath made little clouds in the clear, cold air as he limped about, blinking in the sunlight while he considered where his project should be sited. High above them flew the bluejay on his journalistic rounds, pausing to sail for a moment on motionless wings so sharply dark against the blue sky that an edge of white showed all around them. The mouse and his child stood dark and still on the white snow. The keen wind whistled through their tin and hummed in the father's unwound spring. The muskrat stood solidly planted on the earth, thinking hard as he looked up with admiration at the tooth marks on the stumps.

'Those beavers may not have intellect,' he said, 'but they've got method.' He began to fuss with sticks and stones, muttering to himself.

'Will it take long?' asked the mouse father.

'Not very long, as these things go,' said Muskrat. Having found a short, thick branch that had fallen during a storm, he was seated astride it, laboriously planing it flat with the heavy axe head.

'Now,' he said, panting from his efforts and puffing out little clouds of misty breath, 'the up-and-down is ready, and we attach the X.' He had split the end of the stubby plank he had fashioned, and now he wedged the short length of broken axe handle into the split so that the cutting edge of the axe was at right angles to the plank.

Muskrat looked up at the tree he had chosen, an aspen not far from the edge of the pond. The tree was two feet thick, and the grey trunk towered sixty feet into the clear sky. He took the little plank with the axe head and balanced it like a seesaw on a rock so that the cutting edge rested against the tree. Then he tied a stone to one end of the plank to weight the axe head, and another heavier stone at the other end for a counterweight.

Now when Muskrat touched the plank the axe head lifted, and when he let it go it came down and bit into the tree with a satisfying CHONK. 'There,' he said. 'It just goes up and down like that until it gnaws down the tree.'

'What will make the X go up and down?' asked the mouse child.

'You will,' said Muskrat, 'and I must say that I envy you your part in this.' He tied a long piece of string to the end of the plank, then led the string under a forked twig that he stuck in the snow like an upside-down Y. He tied the free end of the string to the mouse father's arm, and he scooped out an oval track in the snow for the mouse and his child to walk in.

'Are you ready?' said Muskrat.

'Yes,' said father and son together.

Muskrat wound up the father, and the mouse and his child walked around the oval track in the snow. The forked twig acted as a pulley for the string, and as they walked away from the tree the plank tilted to lift the axe; as they walked back towards the tree the axe fell with a CHONK.

'Well,' said Muskrat. 'Why times How will, in time, equal What. There we are. That's it!'

'How long will it take to fell the tree?' asked the mouse child, backing around the oval as his father pushed him.

'Let me see,' said Muskrat. 'This is late winter, and the tree is about thirteen X's around the trunk. Once around the track equals once up and down equals CHONK!' His voice trailed off into a low mumble as he calculated. 'We'll get it done by late spring,' he said. 'Easily.'

'Late spring!' said the father. 'Does it take the beavers that long?'

'No,' said Muskrat. 'But of course they have the tools, you see, and we must use makeshifts.'

'What a long time to walk in a circle!' said the mouse child.

'It's an oval,' said Muskrat. 'Don't think of the walking. Think of the crash; think of the splash; think of the ever-widening ripples!'

The mouse and his child walked steadily around the oval while the axe rose and fell, its blade biting into the tree with a CHONK, CHONK, CHONK that sent echoes ringing across the pond. As they walked the muskrat moved the plank and the rock closer to the tree, so that the axe

progressively bit deeper; and when the cut was well started he moved the whole apparatus around to a new part of the trunk. Then he made a new oval track in the snow for the mouse and his child.

'Do you suppose,' the father asked Muskrat, 'that while we walk you might begin to think about self-winding?'

'Ah!' said Muskrat. 'That's not pure thought, you know; that requires some tinkering. I can't consider the Hows and the Whats of your clockwork without taking you apart; and I can't take you apart until we've finished our work here.'

'In the late spring,' said the father.

'That's right,' said Muskrat. 'But the time always passes quickly on an exciting project like this. You'll be done before you know it.'

He looked up as the bluejay reporter passed overhead, circled, and came back. 'Very good,' said Muskrat; 'our work has already begun to attract attention. Good morning!' he called to the jay. 'I'll be happy to give you a brief statement.'

'Later,' said the reporter. 'I have a lot of ground to cover.'

'Have you seen an elephant or a seal?' called the child.

'Don't remember,' said the bluejay. 'MUSKRAT, WIND-UPS ACTIVE IN WINTER SPORTS,' he announced in a less than front-page voice, and flapped away.

*

Day after day the muskrat and the mouse and his child worked at the tree, until the overlapping oval tracks radiated from the trunk like the petals of a flower, and in every oval the tin feet of father and son had worn away the snow until they walked on the bare earth.

While Muskrat's project trudged ahead, the life of the pond went on as always: the beavers were busy in their lodge with production plans for spring; the fish moved slowly in the dark water beneath the ice, and turtles, snakes, and frogs slept through the winter in the mud at the bottom. On the shore the chipmunk and the groundhog slept the season out in burrows down below the snow, while the wood mouse and the rabbit foraged through the frozen nights pursued by owl and fox and weasel. High in the glittering sky Orion the Hunter shone down on the hunted who ran their nightly race and left their tracks for each day's morning sun to see, a record in the snow of who had lived and who had not. Above the mouse and his child waxed and waned the icy moon, and bright Sirius kept his track across the sky while they trod theirs below.

And beyond the beaver pond the world went its way. The Caws of Art decided not to attempt *The Last Visible Dog* again that season. Having lost both their rabbit and their repertory, they recruited a stagestruck opossum and patched together a revue with which they continued their tour. In the meadow and along the stream new regiments of shrew soldier-boys marched and drilled and took up arms for territory. At the dump the broken carousel still played, and rats caroused along the midway as before. The dolls' house, ravaged as it had been by a nursery fire that started when its youthful owners played with matches, became in its romantic ruined state a trysting place for young rat lovers, then a social and athletic club. Of the ladies and the gentlemen all that remained was the globe the scholar doll had had beneath his hand, and that was now a football for the rats. Elsewhere in the dump the gambling dens and dance-halls prospered as before. The sexton beetle and other small businessmen enjoyed full profits for a change, and trade throve unassisted, for Manny Rat had not returned to claim his share. His forage squad stood leaderless in rusting immobility, and at the beer-can avenue's end his television cabinet gaped emptily at the distant fires.

Starting from the pine woods where the weasels had given

up the chase, the frustrated rat, bitten, torn, and generally smarting and stinging from his theatrical debut, went back to where he had last seen the mouse and his child. From there he cast about in ever-widening circles, but found no track or trace of them. He was sorely perplexed and troubled, and growing ever more doubtful of the quest to which he found himself committed. It had begun simply enough: two tin mice had made a fool of him, and he, in order to maintain his self-respect, was bound to smash them. Then, just as the whole affair had reached the point of final resolution, the frog had made a fool of him again, and had taken off his rightful victims with the shrews. By then it had become clear to Manny Rat that nothing was simple any more, but sheer tenacity had driven him upon his third humiliation, in the role of Banker Ratsneak.

He grew morose, and felt himself half overcome by funk. Why must he go on pursuing clockwork mice, he asked himself. Why must he travel all the night, and sneak through thorns and brambles in the daylight, studious to avoid the bluejay's eye? And what would his reward be at the end? By the time he smashed these trumpery windups his name would be forgotten at the dump, his enterprises taken over by younger, upward-moving rats. The frog's words came into his mind: 'A dog shall rise; a rat shall fall.' Were dogs to track *him* down?

But Manny Rat had no choice left; some force beyond himself was pulling him whichever way his quarry turned. He wound the elephant, cursed forlornly at the now empty provision bags she carried, and shuffled on as if at the end of an invisible chain by which his prey would drag him to his doom.

And in another part of that world beyond the pond, high in a hickory tree, in a leafy squirrel nest into which he had providentially fallen when he slipped out of his woollen glove and the horned owl's talons, the frog, under a kind of polite duress that amounted to house arrest, told fortunes night and day, and begged the squirrels to help him down and on his way.

The mouse and his child worked through the winter rains and snows while Muskrat hovered near to wind and oil them and to shift his tree-cutting machinery as necessary. The project was interrupted only when hunger or fatigue forced

him to abandon briefly the world of applied thought for the physical refreshment of the thinker. Lessons were suspended indefinitely, and the young muskrats of the pond enjoyed a holiday, while father and son walked their ovals night and day. Sometimes the work stopped when a storm buried the mouse and his child in snow, and Muskrat had to dig them out; sometimes the father's clockwork froze, and Muskrat would take him and the child back to his den until they were warm enough to work again.

Most of their fur was gone by now, and what was left was long past mildew, and sprouting moss. Their whiskers were blackened and draggled; their rubber tails had lost their snap; their glass-bead eyes were weatherworn and dim, and the last shreds of the blue velveteen trousers flapped forlornly about their legs. The father's motor, so often wet in rain and snow, had stiffened somewhat despite the oiling. Pushing his son backwards around the track, he walked more slowly than before, his eyes fixed on the coin that swung from the child's neck with the drum.

'That coin grows heavier each day,' he said. 'It's hard enough to keep going without pushing any additional weight.'

'It belonged to Uncle Frog,' the child said. 'Maybe it will bring us luck.'

'It didn't bring *him* luck,' replied the father. 'And in any case, I fear that we shall soon be beyond the reach of any luck that may be forthcoming. At this rate our motor will be quite worn out long before we attain self-winding.'

A white mist rose up from the melting snow; the ice had vanished from the pond; the water shivered in the chilly air. The dark earth reeked of spring; the oval tracks were scored in mud. The calling of the crows upon the east wind had the sound of winter's passing. High overhead there flew two northbound Canada geese. Their honking seemed to fall in silent, frozen crystals of encapsulated sound that melted on the warming earth below, releasing, quiet, small, and clear, the voices and their message. The geese swung low, turned upwind, landed on the pond, and rocking on the water, moored to their reflections.

Onwards walked the mouse child, backwards, in his oval track that was only the old and endless circle made more narrow. He followed his own footsteps going nowhere, his one reward the tension of the string as he moved outward from the tree, the chonking bite as he returned to see the axe blade fall again. The thick base of the aspen, marked by thousands of axe strokes, tapered sharply inward to the point on which it balanced.

'Soon!' said Muskrat. 'Very soon now, our project will reach completion. I must plan the final X-strokes so the tree will fall with maximum splash.' He looked about him moodily. 'Then, perhaps,' he said, 'there'll be some notice taken.'

Certainly very little notice had been taken so far. The animals around the pond were fully occupied in living, dying, or waiting, dormant, for the spring. Only the birds had time to watch the project: chickadees told one another to come and see, see, see; cardinals whistled sharply at it; and nuthatches, upside down and busy pecking for grubs on the aspen trunk, said, 'Ha, ha,' as the axe strokes rang out on the cold air.

'You may laugh,' said Muskrat to a nuthatch, 'but you'll see something soon.' He retired to his den for lunch, and the mouse and his child, left to themselves, walked their track until the father's spring ran down.

'It must be soon,' the father said. 'We have been patient for a long time.'

'And then, self-winding!' said the child, and as he spoke he saw two dark figures in the white mist rising from the melting snow. Passing into and out of sight among the bare, black trees and stumps, they came towards the mouse and his child.

Manny Rat still bore the scars of his brief thespian career, and his paisley dressing gown hung all in tatters. He was thinner and sharper-looking than before, and seemed to be thrust forward through the fog by all the darkling midnights that had brought him to this grey and misty morning. He bent to the trail with such concentration that he did not see the father and son until he was almost upon them. Then he lifted up his head, and his smile was that of someone who, after long and painful separation, finds his dearest friends.

The elephant moved slowly. Nothing had been able to force a daytime word from her, nor did she any longer speak between midnight and dawn; in silence she plodded at her master's heels and endured her shame. What was left of her blackened plush was streaked with rust; her one ragged ear had heard no good word for a long time; her one glass eye looked out at life askance.

'Look!' said the child. 'The elephant! We've found her, Papa!' He had never been so happy, had never felt so lucky. He had never doubted that he would make his dream come true, and all remaining difficulties shrank before him now – the dolls' house and the seal would certainly be found, the territory won, and he should have his mama. And then it came to him that Manny Rat was there to take away the whole bright world and smash him.

The elephant was completely overwhelmed. Until now

she had thought only of herself and the injustice done her; the child and the father had been nothing to her. But now into her one glass eye there rushed the picture in its wholeness of the foggy day, the steaming snow, the black trees, the tired father, the tiny, lost, and hopeful child. A world of love and pain was printed on her vision, never to be gone again.

The father could not find a word to say. The sight of the elephant and the rat flashed upon him with such intensity that he seemed to *hear* the seeing of them; his ears crackled and roared, and the two figures expanded in the centre of his vision while all else blurred away. The elephant was shabby and pathetic; her looks were gone, departed with the ear, the eye, the purple headcloth and her plush. The father saw all that, and yet saw nothing of it; some brightness in her, some temper finer than the newest tin, some steadfast beauty smote and dazzled him. He wished that he might shelter and protect her, and all the time he saw the rock uplifted in the paws of Manny Rat. He fell in love, and he prepared to meet his end.

Manny Rat sighed with immense relief as his world spun out of chaos into order once again. Large ease and happiness were his once more; the headache that had plagued him recently was gone. He drew closer with his rock, but his curiosity for the moment overcame his desire to smash the nightmarishly durable father and son. 'Winter sports, eh?' he said. 'What in the world are you doing? It's absolutely fascinating. Good heavens!' he said. 'You're chopping down that great, enormous tree. What a crash that'll make when it goes! How much longer do you think it'll take?'

'What does it matter now?' said the father.

'I *must* see the outcome of this,' said Manny Rat. 'Let's speed things up a little.' He put down his rock, seized the string that was tied to the father's arm, and ran full speed around the track, dragging the mouse and his child along with him while the axe struck faster and faster, its echoes ringing out across the pond.

A long shiver ran up the grey trunk of the aspen to the topmost branches bare against the sky. Slowly at first, then faster, leaving empty sky behind it, the tree leaned earthward with a rending groan, tore one by one its final splinters loose, and fell.

Muskrat had intended to direct the last strokes of the axe so that the tree would fall into the pond in a place where no damage would be done. But now as the aspen toppled it struck a taller tree that had been split by lightning, which fell in turn against a giant that stood dead and rotting at the water's edge. One after another they crashed and fell, and the last one landed squarely on the beaver dam and smashed it. A great splash went slowly up into the air as the saplings were scattered like matchsticks and the waters of the pond poured out into the valley.

The Canada geese took off in a flurry of great beating wings as the water rushed away. The beavers shot out of their lodge, surfaced in a welter of broken twigs and splintered branches, and grasped the situation at once. 'There goes the pond!' they yelled. 'After it, men!' Jeb and Zeb, drawn backwards in a foaming rush of water, shouted, 'No more school for ever!' as they shot the falls, while startled fish on all sides cried, 'The world has sprung a leak!'

The pure-and-applied thinker, dining underground in his den, felt the earth shake. The fireflies went dark with fright, and Muskrat, stumbling through the clutter, limped up to the daylight. The sun had come out through the overcast to burn away the morning mist. The sky was clear; the air was soft with spring. He looked out on a broad expanse of rank-smelling mud, debris, and matted grasses by a tiny, trickling stream where once the pond had been, and while he stood and gazed the bluejay, passing overhead, called down, 'What's new?'

Muskrat pointed to the desolation. 'Why times How equals What,' he murmured.

'Pond minus Dam equals Mud,' replied the jay as he flew off. 'That's not news.'

SIX

MANNY RAT had let go of the string as the tree fell, but the mouse and his child were tied to it. When the top of the aspen struck the ground, the butt of the trunk lifted, caught the string, and flung father and son far out over the pond and into the outward-rushing waters. 'Wait!' yelled Manny Rat, but they were gone. He felt a sudden pang, and knew that somehow he was going to miss them. His life seemed oddly empty, purposeless, and poorer.

The elephant stood facing the pond, her single eye fixed on the place where the mouse and his child had disappeared. Convulsive, racking sobs were shaking her; she wept as if her spring would break, and still weeping, was wound and started homeward to the dump.

Manny Rat was certain that the mouse and his child had gone to the bottom of the pond, and he assumed that as it emptied they would be buried in the mud, never to be seen again. But the father and son had fallen into a floating tangle of sticks and branches, and on it they shot through the broken dam and downstream through the little valley, tossing on the flood.

Half submerged on their flotsam raft, the mouse and his child raced on. Sunlight and shadow, rocks and trees and snags flashed into and out of their vision as their heads bobbed out of the icy water and went under again. Plunging over falls, bumping in the shallows, whirling through all the bends of the stream, they sped on until the flood, having run the length of the valley, poured itself into another pond, miles from where the tree had fallen.

The water rose to overflow the banks and run off into the

surrounding marsh, the raft spun in the eddies, and the good-luck coin, whipped out centrifugally to the length of its string, pulled the mouse and his child off into the deep water. For a moment the nutshell drum kept them afloat; then the strap slipped over the child's head and they sank to the bottom, the brass coin winking into darkness with them.

The broken reflections of trees and sky settled once more into mirrored stillness, across which moved slow ripples from the little bobbing drum. And below the ever-widening ripples, on the bottom with its bitter smell of darkness, of lost boots and old bottles, of rotting leaves and waving green water plants, the mouse and his child stuck headfirst in the mud.

'What happened?' said the child, his words bubbling into the mud and up through the murky water.

'What happened indeed!' said the father. 'Why times How equalled What, and here we are, no closer to self-winding than before!'

'And we've lost the elephant again, right after finding her!' said the child. 'We never even had a chance to say a word to her!'

The father did not answer, but he sent a long and heavy sigh gurgling into the mud.

'Earliness,' said a voice that boomed and quivered in the

deeps. It was a slow and heavy voice, and the sound of it was like the sound of gravel sliding from an iron bucket. 'Earliness in the sense of untimely awakening,' it said, 'See above. One arises to consider the corporeal continuity of AM.' The voice came closer. 'One becomes aware of appetizing aspects of IS. *Which see.*' KLOP! A pair of sharp and horny jaws closed on one of the mouse father's legs. '*Note well,*' said the voice. '*In the work cited.* Inedible.'

'Get us out of the mud, please,' gurgled the father, 'and stop bending my leg.'

'If you're capable of speech, you're capable of being eaten,' said the voice. KLOP! The jaws opened and closed again on the mouse father's leg. '*Compare,*' said the voice. '*In the same place.* Still inedible. Very well then, let us talk.'

'What is there to say when one's head is in the mud?' said the father.

'What is there *not* to say!' came the answer from the gravelly voice. 'The relation of self to mud is basic to any discussion of TO BE. Basic. At the bottom.'

'Our heads are at the bottom,' said the mouse child. 'We're upside-down.'

'The upside-downness of self,' said the voice. 'A good beginning. Continue.'

'We cannot continue,' said the father, 'unless we are put back on dry land and wound up.'

' "Wound up"?' said the voice. 'Define your terms.'

'I don't want to,' said the father. 'I don't like this sort of talk.'

'What other sort of talk is there?' said the voice. 'Here below the surface one studies the depths of TO BE, as manifest in AM, IS, and ARE. And if you don't hold up your end of the conversation I may very well snap you in two even though I don't choose to eat you.'

'We ARE upside-down,' said the father.

'We want TO BE right-side up,' said the child.

'*For example*,' said the voice, and the jaws again closed on the mouse father's leg, more gently than before. He and the child were lifted up and set down first in a whirling cloud of mud particles. The cloud drifted off into the dark, the mud settled, and they found themselves face to face with an enormous snapping turtle who started at them with a savage fixity of concentration. His shell was covered with waving moss and green algae. He was very old and ponderously fat, and the eye that watched them seemed the very eye of time itself, set like a smoky grey jewel in some old and scaling rock. His beaked head swayed before them, snakelike, striking right and left to punctuate his remarks.

'It is undoubtedly a great pleasure for you,' he said, 'to meet C. Serpentina, thinker, scholar, playwright – voice of swamp and pond . . .' He paused to snap up a sleepy frog that had risen from the mud. CHOMP. CHOMP. CHOMP. ULP. 'And the jaws and stomach as well,' he continued. His words ascended to the surface in a string of bubbles, and each one made a silver circle as it burst in sunlight.

'How do you do,' said the father. 'Mouse and Son.'

'To return to our discussion,' said Serpentina. ' "Wound up," you said. In what sense?'

'In the sense of the key in my back,' said the father.

Serpentina looked at the key. 'What does it do?' he asked.

'Key times Winding equals Go,' said the child.

'Go?' said the snapping turtle. 'Go where? This mud being like other mud, we may assume that other mud is like this mud, which is to say that one place is all places and all places are one. Thus by staying here we are at the same time everywhere, and there is obviously no place to go. Winding, therefore, is futile.' Serpentina settled himself comfortably in the ooze, and dismissed the subject of winding from his mind.

'Then how are we to find the elephant again, and the seal?' said the child, and he began to cry.

'We must get out of here,' said the father.

'One has no need to get out of here,' said Serpentina. 'One is at home on the bottom. One sees below the surface of things. One thinks in depth and acquires profundity, the *without which nothing* of ...' SCRUNCH! A fish had swum near him, and he struck with terrible, snaky swiftness. CHOMP, CHOMP, CHOMP, ULP. 'Contemplation,' he said, finishing the sentence and the fish together.

'What do you contemplate?' asked the child.

'Infinity, mostly.'

'What is infinity?'

'*Which see*,' said Serpentina. He turned father and son so that the child found himself facing a tin can that stood upright, half buried in the mud. BONZO Dog Food, said the white letters on the orange label, and below the name was a picture of a little black-and-white spotted dog wearing a chef's cap and apron. The dog was walking on his hind legs and carrying a tray on which there was another can of

Bonzo Dog Food, on the label of which another little black-and-white spotted dog, exactly the same but much smaller, was walking on his hind legs and carrying a tray on which there was another can of Bonzo Dog Food, and so on until the dogs became too small for the eye to follow.

The can had been at the bottom of the pond for a long time, and some of the dogs had dissolved in bits and shreds of coloured paper that drifted off into the dark water. Tiny organisms bloomed on the label, and snails and little flat-worms journeyed boldly from the small print at the bottom to the large letters at the top, grazing contentedly upon the rotting paper.

'Infinity,' said Serpentina with a proprietary air. 'There's no end to it. There comes a time when each of us must contemplate it.' He struck at the empty water two or three times for emphasis.

'My son is only a child,' said the father. 'Let me do it.'

'One can't begin too young,' said Serpentina. 'The child is father to the mouse. *Note well*,' he said, his voice resounding in the depths: 'an endlessness of little dogs, receding through progressive diminution to a revelation of the ultimate truth.'

'Where?' asked the mouse child.

'*In the same place*,' said Serpentina, '*in the work cited. Beyond the last visible dog.*'

'It's odd that you should say that,' said the father. 'There is a play by that name.'

'I am the author of that play,' said the turtle, snapping his jaws dangerously close to the father's head. 'C. Serpentina. Oneself. No doubt you find it astonishing that a thinker of my depth should have conceived anything so light and di-verting, so riotously entertaining, so *popular* in its appeal.'

'There was certainly a great deal of excitement about it the night we saw it performed,' said the father tactfully. 'It

brought the audience to their feet right from the very beginning.'

'That doesn't surprise me in the least,' said Serpentina,
'Furza and Wurza representing as they do the very ISness of
TO BE, cloaked in fun and farce.'

'Quite true,' agreed the father. 'Do you suppose you might
help us out of this pond after we've finished with infinity?'

'For shame!' roared Serpentina. 'Each of us, sunk in the
mud however deep, must rise on the propulsion of his own
thought. Each of us must journey through the dogs, beyond
the dots, and to the truth, alone.' Having said which, he dug
himself into the mud, closed his grey eyes and went to
sleep.

'How are we going to get out of here?' the mouse child
asked his father.

'I don't know,' said the exasperated father. 'We are helpless, as always.' A bit of Muskrat's string, still tied to his arm,
floated upwards to remind him of their vain hopes at the
beaver pond.

'Didn't Uncle Frog once say that the bottom was
strangely close to the top?' said the child.

'This one isn't,' said the father. 'We're in very deep water.
Can you see anything beyond the last visible dog? It isn't fair
to burden you with this sort of thing, but I've got my back
to it.'

'The child is father to the mouse,' said the child. 'I'll do it.'
He examined the BONZO can. 'There's the first dog,' he said,
'and the one after that and the one after that.'

*

Unable to turn away, the mouse child stared at the can as
the days passed. He felt himself grow dizzy as the dogs un-
dulated before him with the motion of the water, but as
hard as he stared, he was never quite certain which dog was
the last one visible.

Winter had left the pond. The trees had lost their bare sharpness, and their branches were blurring into leaf. Skunk cabbages pushed their coarse green points up out of the black, boggy earth, and the nights grew clamorous with spring peepers. Robins were hard at work among the earthworms; the rattling cry of the kingfisher sounded along the banks; mallards cruised among the reeds; and from the surrounding swamps came the whistle of the marsh hawk and the pumping of the bittern. The fish that swam past the mouse and his child moved more swiftly now, and the sunlight filtering through the depths seemed warmer than before. Grown frogs and young tadpoles, newts, snakes, and turtles, awakening from hibernation, swam up to the surface as spring came to the pond.

'There's *that* little dog, and the one after that,' said the child; but no matter how hard he tried, he always lost his place among the dogs before he found the last one that the eye could see.

'Maybe I could help you look,' said a small and gentle voice, 'and maybe you'd talk to me and not eat me up. Would you, do you think, not eat me?'

'We don't eat anybody,' said the mouse child. 'Where are you?'

'Here,' said the voice, 'by your feet. I don't have anyone to talk to. It's depressing.'

'Who are you?' said the father.

'I don't know,' said the voice. 'I don't even know *what* I am. When I talk to myself I call myself Mudd. That's silly, I know, but you have to call yourself something if you've got no one else to talk to.' There was a stirring in the ooze at the mouse child's feet, and an ugly little creature rose up and leaned lightly against his leg. 'What are you?' it said.

'We're toy mice,' said the child. 'Is it Miss or Mr Mudd? Please excuse my asking, but I can't tell by looking at you.'

'Miss,' said the little creature. She was something like a misshapen grasshopper, and was as drab and muddy as her name. 'I'll be your friend if you'll be mine,' she said. 'Will you, do you think? I'm so unsure of everything.'

'We'll be your friends,' said the child. 'We're unsure too, especially about the little dogs.'

'I know,' said Miss Mudd. 'It's all so difficult. And of course everyone bigger than I tries to eat me, and I'm always busy eating everyone smaller. So there isn't much time to think things out.' As she spoke she flung what looked like an arm out from her face, caught a water flea, and ate it up. 'It's distasteful,' she said. 'I know it's distasteful. I've got this nasty sort of huge lip with a joint in it like an elbow, and I catch my food with it. And the odd thing, you see, is that I don't think that's how I really am. I just can't believe that I'm this muddy thing you see crawling about in the muck. I don't *feel* as if I am. I simply can't tell you how I feel inside! Clean and bright and beautiful – like a song in the sunlight, like a sigh in the summer air. Do you ever feel that way?'

'Ah!' sighed the father. How could he say how he felt? Far different from the tin mouse who had danced under the Christmas tree certainly, but less than whatever it was he needed to be, hoped to be, and now almost despaired of ever being. His works were clogged with mud and dirt and rust; his spirit was heavy in him.

'I've lost my place again,' said the child.

'I'll help you,' said Miss Mudd. 'I'll point to each dog as you go. There,' she said as she climbed up the side of the can and clung to the label. 'Now I'm at the first dog.'

'And the one after that and the one after that,' said the mouse child, while Miss Mudd changed her position accordingly and pointed to the appropriate dog.

All through the lengthening days of spring the mouse child looked at the BONZO label. Water plants put out their roots and anchored to him; little colonies or algae settled on him, flourished, and increased; snails fed on the last scraps of his fur; catfish nibbled at his whiskers, and still he sought the last visible little black-and-white spotted dog. The father, his eyes fixed always on his son, saw the words YOU WILL SUCCEED disappear as the good-luck coin turned green, then black. The child's glass-bead eyes grew ever dimmer and more tired while the father watched helplessly, infinity at his back.

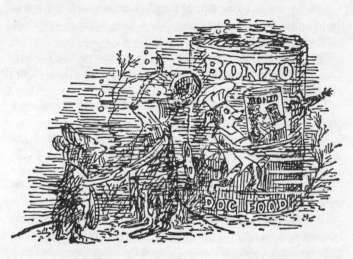

Springtime passed. The flickering play of shadows from the leaves above dappled the depths below, and the mud on the bottom smelled of summer. Water striders darted on silver points of light far above the heads of the mouse and his child, and fish leaped after hovering mayflies, to fall back with bright splashes that spangled the quivering water ceiling.

'Have you found it yet?' the mouse father asked the child. He felt his clockwork stiffening inside him with long disuse, and as all hope of getting out of the pond faded, he found himself thinking that the mud, once one got used to it, was not uncomfortable; the motion of the water was soothing. The startling, sudden, lightning-bright image of the elephant in the mist of that departed morning was sharp within his memory, and it was painful to him, as if a spring within his mind were wound up achingly tight. Powerless to act, he could not convert that coiled energy to motion, and his determination faded as he settled deeper in the mud.

'If Why times How equals Dog,' said the child, who was thoroughly confused by now, 'then Dog divided by How must equal Why.'

Two passing tadpoles swam between him and the BONZO can, where they encountered a water snake. 'This way, please,' said the snake, and swallowed them.

'It looks bad,' said one of the tadpoles as they disappeared down the snake's throat.

'You never know,' said the other. 'If we can just get through this, maybe everything will be all right.'

'Keep your eyes on the dogs,' said Miss Mudd to the mouse child. 'Let us persevere even though the prospects are uncertain.'

The water was especially clear that day, and the BONZO label sharp and well defined. To the mouse child the endless dogs no longer seemed to be printed on the paper label of a tin can. He felt them to be real and alive – a pack of ancient brothers through which his spirit, projected from his seeking eyes, ranged forward on its journey. As in a dream he felt himself move on from one dog to the next until he saw, with sudden and shocking clarity, the last and smallest little dog still recognizable as dog. Beyond that were only tiny dots of colour. Still the child stared, and saw between the dots of colour blank white space, emptiness that seemed to flow back towards him from the smallest dog out through the largest.

'Nothing,' said the mouse child. 'I can see the nothing between the dots. Nothing at all, coming and going. Nothing is what is beyond the last visible dog.'

KLOP! C. Serpentina rose up from the mud and snapped his jaws. 'Nothing!' he said. 'Absolutely nothing! Accretions and abstractions of annotated nothing. Bafflements of nothing. Charismas, demiurges, and epiphanies of nothing. *Note well. See above. See below*: Nothing.' SCRUNCH! CHOMP, CHOMP, CHOMP. ULP, ULP. He had snapped up the snake that had eaten the tadpoles, and was a long time in swallowing it.

'Nothing!' said the mouse father. 'What about the ultimate truth?'

'That's it,' said Serpentina. 'Nothing is the ultimate truth.'

'Nothing?' said the child.

'Nothing,' repeated Serpentina.

'Oh, I shouldn't like to think that,' said Miss Mudd, dodging quickly away from the snapper's jaws. 'It scarcely seems fair, does it? Of course, I'm not really sure.'

'I don't believe it,' said the mouse child. The coloured dots were dancing in his vision; the dogs seemed to surround him. He felt his mind leap, as Muskrat's had when he conceived the X. 'I wonder what's on the other side of nothing?' he said.

'Tiny upstart!' said Serpentina. 'Who are you to seek the other side of nothing?'

'If I'm big enough to stand in the mud all this time and contemplate infinity,' said the child, 'I'm big enough to look at the other side of nothing.'

'Even *I* am,' said Miss Mudd. She reached out her jointed lip, tore off the last visible dog, and began to chew it up.

'That's cheating,' rumbled Serpentina, missing again as he struck. 'You can't swallow infinity.'

'I just want to see what's behind it,' said the child. '*In the work cited*. That's fair, isn't it?'

'Very well,' said Serpentina. 'Develop your premise.' He retired once more into the ooze and went to sleep.

Miss Mudd chewed and swallowed steadily. As the paper of the label disappeared, the shiny tin behind it became visible, and the child saw a beady eye looking at him from the surface of the can. Gradually the area of exposed tin widened, and he saw his own face and his out-stretched hands holding his father's hands. His reflection in the counter he had stood on long ago had been below his field of vision; he had never seen himself before, but he recognized his father, and therefore knew himself. 'Ah,' he said, 'there's nothing on the other side of nothing but us.' Miss Mudd looked at herself in the tin, then covered her face and turned away.

The mouse child felt himself fanned by a current of water as a large-mouth bass swam past him and glowered at the tin can. 'Move along buddy,' the fish said to his own reflection. 'I'm nesting here.'

'You're talking to yourself,' said Miss Mudd, stepping aside as the bass struck at her.

Unconvinced, he backed water slowly, saw that the other fish did the same, and withdrew. 'And *stay* away!' he said over his shoulder as he left.

'They're big and strong, but they're silly,' said Miss Mudd. 'Shiny things on strings are always coming down to catch them.'

The child looked at their reflection in the shining tin, and in the hands that held his own he felt his father's grip grown weak. 'There's nothing beyond the last visible dog but us,' he said. 'Nobody can get us out of here but us. That gives us Why. Now we have to figure out the Hows and the Whats.'

'I fear that Serpentina is right,' said the father. 'Nothing is the ultimate truth, and this mud is like all other mud.'

'I don't care if it is,' said the child. 'I want to get out of here. Can you find some string?' he asked Miss Mudd.

'Oh, yes,' she said. 'There's a lot of it here on the bottom. It gets caught in snags. I'll get some right away.'

The child stood muttering to himself while his father stared beyond him into the empty water and Serpentina snored in the mud. 'Up times Down,' said the mouse child. 'In divided by Out. Here into There.'

'Here I am with the string,' said Miss Mudd, returning through the ooze with one end of a fishing line in her mouth. 'I've got quite a long piece of it. Will it do, do you think?'

'Yes,' said the mouse child. 'And now I must have silence, so I can work out Mouse's Much-in-Little.'

Far above him the sunlight drowsed on the water; the shadows flickered in the leaves, and the song of the cicadas vibrated on the warm air like the sound of summer's clockwork running down.

Hours passed, and it was midday when Miss Mudd's ugly little face appeared among the reeds and lily pads where the nutshell drum still floated quietly by the edge of the pond. She clung tiredly to the reed stem she had climbed, a length of fishing line hanging straight down from her jaws into the water. With what seemed the last of her strength she hauled up the end of the line with the good-luck coin attached. She ate up the algae that had covered it, and scrubbed it as well as she was able. Now, although it was not bright, the brass was capable of glimmering in the water, and she hoped it would suffice. YOU WILL SUCCEED ... YOUR LUCKY DAY IS ... said the alternating legend as the coin twisted on its string. Dragging it on to a lily pad, Miss Mudd left it there among the loose coils of line, then climbed down the reed stem and disappeared below the surface.

In an hour or so she reappeared, more line in her jaws, on the rocks near the bank, where a row of painted turtles lay basking in the sun. Risking her life as she passed each turtle, Miss Mudd crept stealthily on until she came to a flat rock overhung by the low branches of the sumac on the bank.

Here she dragged the line through a narrow fork in one of the branches, then staggered on across the lily pads to where the nutshell drum still rocked in the ripples among the reeds. Working more and more slowly, she tied the end of the line to the strap of the drum. Then she took the end of the line coiled on the lily pad, tied it also to the drum strap, and pushed the coin into the water. The nutshell drum went under, then bobbed up again. Peering down through the water, Miss Mudd saw the coin swinging below her, its worn brass gleaming faintly, like a forlorn hope.

'There,' she said, 'that's it,' and she collapsed, exhausted, on the lily pad. 'I feel so odd!' she said. 'I can scarcely catch my breath, and my eyes are growing dim. Perhaps I'm dying, and my little muddy life is finished, and I never was meant to be anything but what I was.'

Miss Mudd began to cry, and as her body heaved it split down the back. 'Oh!' she said, and felt the life stir in her wet and wrinkled wings that were already stiffening for flight. 'It was so difficult to be sure!' she sighed. She climbed out of the empty, muddy shell of her discarded self, a dragonfly now, new and lovely, emerald green. She waited patiently until the sun had dried her iridescent wings, then launched herself uncertainly to fly. Her shabby nymphhood crouched forgotten on the lily pad; her old name was forgotten too, and all that lay below the surface in the dark. Glittering above the pond she flew away, lilting on the warm wind like a song in the sunlight, like a sigh in the summer air.

In the mud at the bottom the mouse and his child waited. The end of Muskrat's string, still tied to the father's arm, was now knotted to the fishing line that hung swaying in a slack curve up to the surface and the forked branch above the flat rock.

'Waiting,' said the child. 'How much of our time we have spent waiting!'

Serpentina awoke, yawned, and snapped his jaws

hungrily. 'One rises afresh,' he said, 'to new investigations of TO BE. What have you found beyond the farther side of nothing?'

'A way out,' replied the mouse child.

'Indeed!' said Serpentina. 'Have you paused to consider that there *is* no way out? Each way out of one situation necessarily being the way into another situation, we may say that – Stop! Pay attention!'

But the mouse and his child, exploding from a cloud of mud, were half-way to the sunlit surface of the pond. Above them, the nutshell drum went slanting down into the water. The bass that had swallowed the coin was off like a bullet, and the line cut a V-shaped wake through the water as it ran smoking over the forked branch and hauled up the long-submerged tin mice.

Sodden and heavy with the silt of the bottom, they broke the surface, burst splashing into the sunlight, and went skittering across the turtle rocks. 'Summer people!' hissed the turtles, and plopped into the water in rapid-fire order. Father and son banged into the narrow fork of the branch, the knot that tied Muskrat's string to the fishing line slipped out, and they dropped with a soggy rattle to the flat stone by the bank.

The mouse and his child lay in a puddle on the stone as the water drained out of them. They were spotted, streaked, and pitted with rust at all their joints, and the arms they stretched out to each other were naked, rusty wires. What fur remained was black with rot, and green with moss and algae. Their tattered ears stood bent and crooked on their heads. Their whiskers hung in limp dejection.

The sunlight seemed intolerably bright, and its warmth on their tin was delightful. Sounds were needle-sharp and clear; they listened to the rustling of the leaves, the drone of the cicadas, the slow, sweet notes of a white-throated sparrow, and a strange, loud sound that came from the marshes that bordered the pond. OONG, BONK, CHOONG! It went, pumping and thumping in the reeds; OONG, BONK, CHOONG! in a steady rhythm. In a nearby birch tree, high above them, a kingfisher watched curiously. In his claws he held a coil of fishing line, one end of which hung straight down into the water. The pounding in the marsh stopped as the child's little tin voice rang out over the pond. 'What shall we do now?' he said.

'Leave quickly, I hope,' said a sepulchral voice from the reeds nearby.

The father, who lay facing the sound, saw that the speaker was a heavyset brown wading bird, streaked and mottled in such a way that as he stood motionless he was almost invisible among the reeds. He stood like a reed too, his long beak pointing straight up. His eyes, however, set very close together like a little pair of yellow spectacles, stared straight ahead glassily at the mouse father.

'Who are you?' said the father, staring back at the bird, who seemed to come and go like an optical illusion.

'One who loves privacy,' replied the bittern. 'Let that suffice. Our acquaintance need go no further. Do not let me detain you. Good-bye.' The wind stirred the reeds, and he swayed with them maintaining his invisibility.

'If you could help us . . .' the child began.

'On your way – I should be delighted,' said the bittern. 'How may I assist your departure?'

'Turn the key in my back and wind us up, please,' said the father.

The bittern left the reeds and waded skulkingly to the stone, as if begrudging the privacy he lost with every step. Holding the father firmly in place with one large foot, he took a strong grip on the key with his beak. His little eyes bulged alarmingly as he strained at it, and his neck twisted half-way around, but not the key. 'What sort of hoax is this?' he said. 'Your key won't turn.'

'We're a little rusty,' said the father. 'Please try again.'

The bittern braced himself once more, took a fresh grip on the key, and grunted heavily as it began to turn. The cogs clicked as the rusty spring tightened inside the father, and he waited for the familiar feeling of release that always followed it. The bittern stood them on their feet and let go of the key. Nothing happened. The father's legs did not move.

'Good-bye,' said the bittern. 'Don't stop to thank me.' And he vanished among the reeds.

'What's the matter, Papa?' said the child. 'Why aren't we moving?'

'We're broken!' said the father, hurt as much by the dreaded word as the painful tightness of his spring inside him.

'Broken!' said the child, too shocked to cry.

'Broken,' repeated the father. 'We have survived bank robbery, war, the Caws of Art, the breaking of the dam, and the contemplation of infinity, only to come to this!'

'Perhaps you still have too much of the pond inside your clockwork,' said the child. 'Perhaps when we've dried out a little . . .'

'Drying out won't be enough,' the father said. 'I can feel that it's more serious than that. Muskrat is our only hope now. But how can we get to him?'

'EXTRA!' screamed a familiar voice above them, and the bluejay flashed into view. 'MUSKRAT KILLED BY FALLING TREE. MEETS DEATH IN BEAVER DAM RECONSTRUCTION PROJECT. LAST WORDS: WHAT DIVIDED BY HOW EQUALS WHY. DIVING BEETLES ROUT BACKSWIMMERS IN WATER POLO. TADPOLES HIT BOTTOM IN LITTLE LEAGUE STANDINGS.' He looked down, nodded in greeting, shouted, 'WINDUPS IDLE,' and flew away.

'Look out!' yelled the kingfisher from the birch tree.

'LUNCHTIME!' shrieked a third and harsher voice. A shadow fell upon the mouse and his child, and they felt the sudden, sharp grip of powerful claws. The whole pond, the trees around it and the marsh, all dropped away below, grew small, and tilted out of sight as father and son rose up into the air in the talons of a marsh hawk. 'Kill!' sang the hawk with great good cheer. His eyes were fierce and yellow; his talons were like steel. 'Kill!' he sang. 'I have a kill! Blood to drink and flesh to tear!' He laughed, and his wings flashed in the sun.

The air was warm and pleasant as they flew; the gentlest of breezes sped the hawk along and sighed and murmured after him. Below smiled sleepy green and yellow fields that wore flashing streams like jewels, while stately trees stood nodding by their own cool shadows. The world had never seemed so fair.

Still waterlogged and heavy from his long immersion, the father hung from the child's hands and felt his own weight dragging at him. He felt his hands, rusty and crumbling, begin to slip away from those that held him. His tight spring ached inside him, and a great longing for peace and rest came over him. 'Why not give up the struggle?' he sighed. 'I can hold on no longer.'

'Don't say that, Papa!' cried the child. 'I've got you! You won't fall!'

'We had our hopes, and they are gone,' said the father listlessly. 'Let me drop into some peaceful meadow where the grass will grow among my scattered clockwork! Why wait to be smashed upon some lonely rock when the hawk finds out we aren't edible!'

'If we'd been edible we'd never have lasted this long,' said the child. Ahead on the horizon hung the smoke of burning rubbish. '*See below*,' he said. 'I think we're heading towards the dump.' He was silent for a few moments. 'Do you remember,' he said, 'that Muskrat told us we'd have to be taken apart before he could figure out the Hows and Whats that would make us self-winding?'

'Yes,' said the father, 'but Muskrat is gone.'

'*We* aren't,' said the child. 'Not yet.'

They were high above the earth, the ground below them tilting in slow sweeps as the hawk soared in an updraft. The mouse child saw the dump in the distance, the railway tracks and the swamp beyond them, the highway, the junkyard, and the roofs of the town. The hawk circled, climbing higher. The child saw something else, and laughed. 'You there!' he said to the hawk.

'What's on your mind?' said the marsh hawk. 'You do a lot of talking for a small-sized kill.'

'What are you having for lunch today?' asked the child.

'The usual thing,' said the hawk. 'Blood to drink and flesh to tear. Yours. I'm just working up an appetite so you'll taste that much better when I get home.'

'Skreep, skreep!' laughed the child.

'What's so funny?' said the hawk.

'You're not going to eat us,' said the child.

'That's how much *you* know,' replied the hawk. 'Didn't anybody ever tell you about the balance of nature? It's like a beautiful pyramid, with a lot of juicy mice and chipmunks down at the bottom and a hawk up at the top. Naturally the hawk eats up the mice and the chipmunks. That's how it is. I eat and you get eaten.'

They were almost over the dump now. The mouse child saw the tin cans glinting in the sunlight. 'That's all very well,' he said, 'but you won't eat us.'

'Yes, I will,' said the hawk, 'and I'll take a little bite right now, just to show you what I mean.' He tore at the tin bodies of father and son, and shrieked with pain as he chipped his beak. 'Ugh!' he said, '*you* aren't part of the balance of nature!' He let them fall from his talons and flew away, shaking his head as he tried to get the taste of rusty tin out of his beak. Down dropped the mouse and his child, turning over and over in the air, the wind whistling through their tin as they plunged to the earth.

They struck with a rattling crash on the tin-can slope that overlooked the fires, and the dump leaped and shuddered in their vision as the impact broke their grip on each other's hands, split their bodies open, and flung them violently apart. The scattered pieces of the mouse and his child lay on the path where once the frog had told their fortune, and they saw and heard no more.

Below them winked red embers through the broken skeletons of umbrellas and the carcasses of old shoes, while flames flew up in wrecked birdcages, singing where silence long had been. Empty bottles and dead light bulbs popped dully, and a stench rose with the drifting smoke and ashes. On the tracks beyond the dump a freight train whistled. The wind sighed over the rubbish mountains.

The rusty clockwork rolled from the wreckage of the father and came to rest nearby. A tiny snail crawled out of it and slowly made his way across the dented scraps of tin. Half of the child lay facing the fires; the other half turned blindly to the sky, where slow clouds drifted in the golden light of late afternoon.

SEVEN

'No peace,' said the bittern as he stomped home through the bogs. 'No quiet. No privacy whatever. The world is constantly at one's door, chattering and squeaking and demanding to be wound up.'

He sighed and went back to the frog pound he had been building before the voices of the mouse and his child had distracted him. Well hidden in the marsh, an unfinished fence of stakes driven into the mud defined an enclosure which, when complete, would provide a place where his dinners might be kept fresh until such time as they were needed.

The bittern approached the stake at which he had left off, jumped on to the flat rock he had been using as a mallet, grasped it firmly with his toes, beat his wings, and lifted the rock as he raised himself into the air. OONG! He grunted, and brought the rock down on the stake. BONK! Then he let his breath out. CHOONG! He repeated the process, pumping and thumping like a small pile driver as the rock went up and down steadily until the stake was driven in among its fellows.

When the fence was complete and the frog pound ready to be stocked, the bittern waded off, his shoulders hunched, his neck in a flattened S-curve, and his long, sharp beak moving crankily forward and back with each step. In a few minutes his little yellow-spectacle eyes brightened as he came upon a large bullfrog, wearing a grease-stained canvas work glove, who sat on a tussock and stared open-mouthed at that part of the sky where the marsh hawk had just passed overhead.

The bittern pointed his beak straight up and swayed invisibly among the reeds while his downward-looking eyes examined the frog minutely. Having judged from the plumpness of the glove that the bullfrog was sufficiently tender for the evening meal, the bittern was about to dart his beak forward at his prey when it spoke.

'STOP!' roared Frog. 'DESTINY IS NOT TO BE TRIFLED WITH. DO NOT COMMIT THE TRAGIC ERROR OF SATISFYING PRESENT APPETITE AT THE COST OF FUTURE FULFILMENT.'

'What's that you say?' asked the bittern, drawing back in alarm.

'AH, MY FRIEND,' bellowed Frog, puffing out his yellow throat and blowing himself up as large as possible, 'TO HOW MANY OF US IS GIVEN THE OPPORTUNITY OF SEIZING THAT PRICELESS

MOMENT IN WHICH THE TANGLED THREADS OF MINGLED FATES CAN BE UNSNARLED AND WOVEN, WARP AND WOOF, INTO THEIR PRE-ORDAINED DESIGN!'

'What?' said the unnerved frogstalker. 'Where? Warp who? Woof what?'

'QUICKLY!' boomed Frog, 'FOLLOW THAT HAWK, AND TAKE ME AS YOUR PASSENGER.' Even as he spoke he rapidly wove a little sling of reeds in which the bird might carry him. It had taken him a long time to find a new glove, and he was taking no chance on slipping out of this one. 'DESTINY DOES NOT WAIT,' he said. 'MAKE HASTE! I SHALL EXPLAIN ALL AS WE TRAVEL.'

*

The bass that had swallowed the good-luck coin swam back to his nesting hollow, the line trailing behind him until the drum caught on a root. Then the knot that tied it to the coin came undone, the line slid out of the fish's throat, the nutshell drum bobbed once more to the surface, and the bass was free. 'Not bad,' he said with a chuckle as he felt the coin's smoothness in his stomach. Highly satisfied with himself, he tidied up his little hollow, patrolled its borders aggressively, inquired of the neighbouring bass whether there had been any messages, then swam off in search of new adventure.

He found it in a quiet corner of the pond, where slanting sunlight came down in long rays through the shadows of the leaves, and something shiny was descending slowly through the water. It was the tin seal at the end of a fishing line, wiggling her tail and flapping her flippers.

The metal rod that once had held the ball was now ornamented with bright feathers that slowly and seductively revolved. Several fishhooks dangled below the feathers, and the seal's worn tin glinted in the green-lit water. Like the mouse and his child, she had long ago broken the clockwork rule of daytime silence, and now she sang softly, as if to herself:

> Just a little lonely maybe,
> Thinking of you only, baby.

'Holy smoke!' said the bass. 'Look at that action!' Churning the water as he worked up speed, he struck, hooked himself, and with the seal, was hauled up out of the pond to the branch of the birch tree where the kingfisher sat. Beside the bird was a string bag that contained his fishing equipment: spare hooks and lines that he had salvaged and a little can of oil with which he kept the seal in operating condition.

'Good work!' said the kingfisher. Stocky, handsome, and sporty looking, with an honest beak, a frazzled crest, and a friendly eye, a bachelor whose love for solitary fishing trips had kept him from ever settling down, he found the tin seal both a charming companion and an efficient helper. He took the bass from the hook and clubbed it to death on the branch. Then he coiled up his line, oiled the seal carefully, and cleaned the fish, putting the coin, when he found it, into the string bag. Then he sat down and enjoyed a hearty lunch.

'Funny thing happened while you were underwater,' he said to the seal. He described the emergence of the mouse and his child from the pond, their winding by the bittern, and their subsequent capture by the hawk.

'Two windup mice,' said the seal. 'Was one big and one little? Blue trousers? Patent leather shoes?'

'One big and one little,' said the kingfisher. 'Their trousers might have been blue a long time ago. No shoes – '

Noticing the nutshell drum floating on the pond below him, he interrupted the conversation to fetch it and add it to his kit.

'Two windup mice,' the seal repeated. 'I wonder if they're the same ones I used to know.' She remembered how the child had cried, not wanting to go out into the world. 'Which way'd the hawk go?' she asked.

'He was heading for home,' said the kingfisher. 'He lives in the swamp on the other side of the dump, across the railway tracks.'

'He can't eat them,' said the seal. 'I wonder if he's dropped them?'

'If he has, we'll probably hear about it on the Late Sports Final,' said the kingfisher. 'Feel like flying over towards the swamp for a look around?'

'Let's,' said the seal. The kingfisher packed his gear, put her into the string bag, and they took off.

*

While the kingfisher and the bittern were following the marsh hawk, another bird was ahead of them, hot on the same trail: the bluejay too had seen the harrier and his prey. Avid for disaster and eager for a headline, he pursued his story at top speed, and was in time to see the mouse and his child fall. The bluejay's shadow glided over the child's broken face as the reporter circled low for a close look at the wreckage, then soared up on the warm air from the fires.

'LATE SPORTS FINAL!' he screamed. 'WINDUPS CRASH IN DUMP. NO SURVIVORS.' The jay scanned the immediate vicinity for late scores, yelled, 'DUNG BEETLES BLANK ROACHES IN FIRST GAME OF DOUBLE HEADER,' and flew away, leaving behind him silence broken only by the crackle of the flames in the burning rubbish.

The kingfisher heard the news, and altered his course to head towards the sound of the bluejay's voice. The frog heard it, and urged the bittern to fly faster. Manny Rat heard it too. He had been looking up at the sky, impatient for the dark, when he saw the hawk drop something over the dump, and now he kept his eye on the spot marked by the blue-jay.

'Iggy!' he called, and Ralphie's successor, an equally ill-favoured young rat of stocky build and no scruples whatever, hurried to his master's side.

'What's up, Boss?' said Iggy.

'Get over to the ridge on this side of the fires,' said Manny Rat, 'and see if you can find a couple of windups.' Iggy saluted and shuffled off as directed.

'It *couldn't* be those two,' mused Manny Rat aloud. And yet he was disquieted; his heart was beating faster, and his head began to ache a little. Months ago, on his return to the dump, he had let it be known that the fugitive windups had been brought to a final accounting after a long and arduous chase, and the reaction of the general public had been one of heightened respect for him. Was he to be made a fool of once again, he wondered? Anxiously he watched the departing figure of his lieutenant, and looked beyond him to the distant tin-can ridge. 'No,' he said again, 'it couldn't be those two. But on the other hand, who else would drop out of the sky like that?' He frowned, and looked across the rubbish mountains to the setting sun.

*

Iggy was still several rubbish piles away when first the kingfisher, then the bittern, landed, stirring up a little cloud of ashes around the debris of the mouse and his child.

'We're too late,' said the seal after the frog had hastily introduced himself and the bittern. 'I'm afraid this is the end of them.'

The frog said nothing, but quickly gathered up the clockwork and the parts of the broken tin bodies and put them into the kingfisher's string bag. Then both birds took off with their passengers and flew to the edge of the dump, where they perched in an oak tree near the railway tracks and considered what to do next.

'Now that I have assisted you with your warps and woofs,' said the bittern to the frog, 'I really must return to my usual mode of life. Good-bye.'

'Good-bye,' said Frog. 'On behalf of my friends and myself, let me offer our heartfelt thanks for your prompt and generous response to my appeal for help.' But the bittern, his farewells completed, stayed where he was, looking at the broken father and son.

'I hope we've got all the pieces,' said Frog. He took the arms and legs and the two halves of the mouse child, and fitted them together, bending the little tin flaps back into place along the edges of his body so that the child would not immediately fall apart.

As his two halves came together the mouse child returned to himself. He heard all at once the rustle of the leaves around him, and saw, reflecting the light of the setting sun, the golden eyes of his old friend fixed anxiously upon him. 'Uncle Frog!' he said. 'I saw you following the hawk; I knew you'd find us before Manny Rat did.'

Frog set him down carefully on the branch and picked up the father. The mouse child had not yet seen the others around him; standing alone, and a little giddy without his father's hands supporting him, he was looking straight ahead out through an opening in the leaves. 'Ours!' he said suddenly and fiercely. 'Our territory!'

'What's he talking about?' said the kingfisher. Then he peered out through the leaves and saw what the child saw.

Between their tree and the railway tracks stood a little cottage, long abandoned. Its paint had flaked away, the empty windows stared out blindly at the tracks, and tall weeds choked the doorway. Beside the cottage was a pole with a wooden platform at the top of it. A large birdhouse had once stood there for purple martins to nest in, but it was gone now. Stark against the red sky, its mansard roof crudely mended with tin and all its chimneys and dormers jammed roughly back in place, was the dolls' house that had been on the counter in the toy store years ago.

The windows had not a pane of glass among them; thick pieces of wood, fastened askew, replaced the ornate mouldings and the graceful balusters and brackets of porches and

balconies. The scrollwork and the carven cornices were gone, and the whole house bristled with bent nails clumsily driven and smashed into the splintered wood. Nothing was straight, and everything awry. Newly fitted to the roof in place of the lost lookout was a crooked watchtower. The hinged front that had once swung open to reveal the interior was nailed shut, and a heavy coat of black paint covered all. Secondhand crêpe-paper bunting, the red, white, and blue of which had run together in rain and damp, festooned the balconies, and little faded flags drooped from the chimneys and the tower.

A clothesline pulley fastened to a branch above the roof showed how the house had been raised; a partly filled sherry bottle hanging from the boom of an Erector-Set crane hinted at a party; and pacing on the watchtower in a new silk dressing gown was Manny Rat. Silhouetted against the sunset, the present master of the dump gazed at the distant rubbish fires and hummed a little tune while he thought with pleasurable anticipation of the house-warming he planned for that evening.

On his return to the dump after his long absence, he had quickly seen the house's possibilities as a private residence, and as quickly had preempted it. The ambitious rat, as he expanded his operations with the fullness of time, had become a considerably more important personage than before: he now commanded squads of rats as well as windups, and he had begun to think of the dignity of his position. The rubbish piles were constantly changing; the television set where he had lived no longer commanded any view whatever. Manny Rat resolved on a dwelling appropriate to his rank, and a location a little removed from the hurly-burly, where he might relax after the cares of the night while yet keeping an eye upon his business interests. Accordingly he evicted the social and athletic club then resident and devoted his ingenuity to the relocation and restoration of his new property. Press gangs of smaller, weaker rats had toiled to raise up and repair the house; the windups of the forage squad had trudged heavy-laden for miles with the materials for its renovation. And the elephant had been harnessed to the crane and windlass so that she might help to put in good order for her master the house she once had called her own.

She stood beside it now, bereft of any plush, her bare tin weatherstained and rusty, her clockwork all but worn out in the service of Manny Rat. Through a glassless window her one eye saw the room in which the lady and gentleman dolls had sat at their tea, where now a garbage buffet set out upon the floor awaited the delectation of the invited rats. Rat servants scuttled up and down stairs, making all ready for the evening, while rat guards armed with spears walked the platform, favouring the elephant with low humour and coarse remarks as they made their rounds.

The father was hastily put together as the son had been, and speechless with relief, he looked into the face of the frog. Then he saw the elephant and the dolls' house. 'Oh!' he said, 'Oh!' again, and wept. Then he felt a great rage growing in him, and he said the same words that the child had spoken: 'Ours!'

'Look, Papa!' said the child as the frog moved the tin seal to where the father and son could see her. 'The elephant, the seal, and the house. It wasn't impossible! We've found them all!'

'And the enemy who awaits us at the end,' said the father, watching Manny Rat upon his black tower. He was silent for a little while. Through the gathering dusk he looked at the forlorn elephant standing by the dolls' house. The road had been long and hard indeed, but now he knew that he had found what he had wanted to find at the end of it. 'Now we must fight for our territory,' he said.

'I don't understand,' said the seal. 'Kingfishers have territories, and I know that animals do. But toys don't.'

'We aren't toys any more,' said the father. 'Toys are to be played with, and we aren't. We have endured all that Frog foretold – the painful spring, the shattering fall, and more. Now we have come to that place where the scattering is regathered.'

'What do you mean?' asked the seal.

'Be my daughter,' said the father.

'Be my sister,' said the child. 'Will you, so we can have a family?'

The tin seal, her hooks and draggled feathers drooping about her head, sat on the branch and looked at the darkening sky. Her past life came back to her all in a rush – the store, the house she had gone to and the children who had broken her, the dump and Manny Rat, her travels with the Caws of Art and the rabbit's flea circus, the quiet days with Muskrat, and her daily work with the kingfisher. On the whole it had not been a bad life, and yet it seemed a long and weary time that she had been alone of her kind in the wide world. She hesitated no longer. 'Yes,' she said, 'I will.'

'Well,' said the bittern, 'it simply is not possible to put off any longer my return to the marsh; I must seek solitude again.' But still he watched and listened curiously, and made no move to go.

'Have you any plan for winning this territory you claim?' Frog asked the mouse and his child.

'Not yet,' said the father.

'I made the hawk drop us here when I saw you following us,' said the child to the frog. 'But I never expected that we'd find the dolls' house and have to fight Manny Rat so soon.'

'As well as seven or eight other rats that I counted in and around the house,' said the bittern, dropping all pretence of leaving, and throwing himself wholeheartedly into the conversation. 'And all the guards, as you may have noticed, are armed.'

'Still,' said the kingfisher, 'someone with a sharp beak, flying fast and striking accurately, might have a sporting chance.'

'Doubtful,' said Frog. 'Very doubtful.'

'There's Manny Rat all alone on the tower,' said the kingfisher, 'and without a spear. What if I got through the guards and finished him off right now?'

'Then all the other rats would move up one,' said Frog, 'and there would be a new Manny Rat to finish off.'

'You're absolutely right,' said the father. 'It isn't simply a matter of killing one rat or winning one battle. That battle must be won in such a way as to inflict upon the enemy a defeat so crushing that every rat in the dump will live in abject terror of us and leave us undisputed masters of that house. Only in that way can we keep our territory once we take it.'

'And relying as we must upon the element of surprise,' said Frog, 'we cannot afford a single wrong move from the very first moment we show our hand.'

'Exactly,' said the father. 'The elephant of surprise. Element,' he corrected himself.

Frog looked out through the leaves into the twilight. Thirty feet away, on the dolls' house platform, the rat guards walked their posts in a sloppy and unmilitary fashion, but seemed quite alert. 'I find myself wondering about those spears,' he said.

As if in answer to his question, one of the guards idly took aim at a swallow that skimmed low over the dolls' house in the dusk. The bird was an easy target, but the rat's marksmanship was poor; the spear barely penetrated a wing covert before it was shaken loose. The guard watched complacently as the scarcely wounded swallow flew up sharply, fluttered brokenly a moment, then dropped like a stone. The guard took another spear from a rack and resumed his round.

'Poison,' said Frog. 'Just as I feared. Friend Rat has learned something from the shrews.'

'What do we do now?' said the kingfisher.

'Wait,' said the father.

'For what, exactly?' asked the bittern.

'I don't know,' the father said, 'but I'll know it when I see it. Something will happen; some sign will indicate the X for

136

us. My son and I have been a long time waiting; we can wait a little longer now that victory is close.' His eyes were fixed on the elephant as he spoke, and there was new energy in his voice.

'How can you be so sure of winning?' asked the seal.

'We have already done our losing,' said the father. 'Our defeats are all behind us.'

Night fell, and a new moon, having risen early, showed its thin yellow crescent now declining in the west. The oak leaves pattered, and with the shifting night breeze came the faint sound of the town hall clock as it struck eight. A dim red glow, as always, lit the sky above the dump, and the sounds of evening, ascending one by one, merged in a general hum and clamour. The carousel played its cracked waltz on the rats' midway; the gambling booths, the gaming dens and dancehalls came noisily to life, then disappeared with all their mingled voice into the lonesome wail and rumble of a passing freight. Above the tracks the green and red lights on the gantry clicked and changed; the engine's headlight slid along the shining rails, picked out leaf and branch and dolls' house where the boss of the dump still paced his tower. The sound grew with the train, as car by clanking car its passage shook the pole and set the dolls' house teetering on the platform. Clacking through the switches went the boxcars, rumbling on until the yellow-windowed caboose and its red lantern dwindled into darkness; the gantry blinked its changes, and the train was gone. An edge of cricket song and silence stayed behind it for a moment in the small and smaller clacking of the rails; then the cracked waltz of the carousel returned, the dancehall's thumping whine, the distant cries of pitchmen and of vendors in the alleyways and tunnels.

By the starlight and the slender moon they could see nothing clearly, but the little group in the oak tree could hear the guards keep watch with steady thump and shuffle as they walked the platform. Several of the off-duty rats lifted their voices in a rowdy song, and two of the servants were squealing insults at each other in a dispute over some mouldy cheese. Father and son listened carefully, focusing their complete attention on every sound in an effort to extract the information that would give them a plan of attack.

There was a clink and rattle in the weeds at the bottom of the pole. Someone had stubbed his toe on something, and was cursing softly. 'Who's that?' challenged Manny Rat.

'It's me – Iggy,' answered his lieutenant. A string ladder rustled as it was let down, and the invisible Iggy climbed up to the platform. A muttered conversation ensued, too low to be audible, and then Manny Rat was heard again, berating his subordinate for his failure to find the fallen windups reported by the bluejay.

The ladder shook again as Iggy descended. They heard him moving about in the weeds, then the unmistakable sound of spring motors being wound up. The forage squad, their collective clockwork set in motion, receded into the distance with Iggy and their song:

> Who's that passing in the night?
> Foragers for Manny Rat!
> We grab first and we hold tight –
> Foragers for Manny Rat!

There was a period of silence in the oak tree. Then the father spoke. 'I think a sign has been given us,' he said.

'What?' asked the child.

'The same one that has been given all along,' said the father. 'The last visible dog.'

'Where?' asked the child.

'On the label of Manny Rat's spare-parts can,' said the father. 'I'm certain that's what rattled in the weeds when Iggy stubbed his toe. In that can we should find the equipment necessary both for fighting Manny Rat and for self-winding. Now all we need is a plan.'

'I think I have a plan,' said the child. 'Did you hear a bobbling sound on the platform when the train went by?'

'Yes,' said the father. 'What about it?'

'Manny Rat repaired the house and painted it and put it up on top of the pole,' said the child. 'But there's one thing he hasn't done yet.'

'What's that?' asked the father.

'He hasn't nailed it down,' replied the mouse child.

The moon had set, and Manny Rat's guests were due to arrive soon. The boss of the dump, awaiting them on the tower of his beautiful new house, stopped his pacing abruptly. Against the background uproar of the dump and the racket of servants and off-duty guards he had become suddenly aware of some unidentifiable sound that was quite close and unspeakably eerie. He strained to hear it again, but it was gone. Manny Rat thought about that horrid sound many times that evening, and when he did, he shivered. But it was only much later that he came to know that what he had heard was the combined hilarity of a kingfisher, a bittern, and a frog, above which rose the peculiar, creaking, squeaking, rattling noise of laughing tin.

EIGHT

MANNY RAT's housewarming was a great success. He had invited the cream of rat society, and all of them attended, twittering and squeaking with high spirits as they climbed the string ladder to the dolls' house. Grizzled old fighters and their plump, respectable wives touched whiskers with gentleman rats grown sleek by cunning and lithe young beauties of vaguely theatrical connection. Debutante rats and dashing young rats-about-town, all the golden youth of the dump, arrived in little laughing groups that achieved an effect of brilliance even in the dark, while doddering dowager rats came escorted by gaunt artistic rats with matted fur, burning eyes, and enormous appetites. Last up the ladder were a scattering of selected social climbers, followed by various hired bravos, obscure ruffians, and cheap hustlers whose good will was worth cultivating.

The hungry guests made a concerted rush for the garbage buffet, and the thirsty ones squealed with delight when they found the sherry bottle, the contents of which were a vicious mixture of the dregs of many bottles. Several of the rats eagerly manned the Erector-Set crane, the punch was swung on to the platform, and the housewarming got under way quickly.

As much as Manny Rat had looked forward to his party, he found his enjoyment flawed by a vague disquietude. It had begun with Iggy's failure to find the windups dropped by the hawk and had intensified with that unearthly laughter out of the night, until now the boss of the dump was nervous and jumpy, and had scant pleasure of the distinguished company assembled under his roof. Having mingled briefly with the guests, he took himself off to his watchtower and paced restlessly above the merriment and the noise.

Beyond the platform quivered the darkness and the night, and Manny Rat knew well that something waited for him there. Back and forth he paced upon the parapet, hearing in the rhythm of his footsteps the words that Frog had spoken long ago in last winter's moonlight: '*A dog shall rise; a rat shall fall.*'

The words were meaningless, he told himself. Undoubtedly it had been Frog's hope that future circumstances, lending themselves at random to the prophecy, should frighten him into a wrong move that would cause his downfall. Manny Rat tried to put that thought out of his mind. There were no dogs rising now to threaten him, nor anything else that he could see. He recalled the wild, weird laughter he had heard, and long and hard he looked into the night from which the sound had come. There was nothing except the dark and rustling mass of the oak tree a few yards distant, nothing but the leaves that whispered in the wind.

Manny Rat did not care for that whispering, and the breeze that stirred the leaves brought to him undertones of scents that baffled and annoyed him. He became less and less happy with the oak tree; he found that he did not like to turn his back to it, and he strained into the darkness, watching and listening for he knew not what. He heard the draggled song of the returning forage squad, the sound of Iggy coming up the ladder, the creak and rattle of the crane that hoisted up the bags unloaded from the windups. Below him in the house the revelry continued, rat-style, in total darkness, its progress marked by shouts, giggles, playful bites, squeals, laughter, and boisterous song, but that which Manny Rat was listening for he did not hear.

He did not hear Frog's stealthy movements in the weeds as

the spare-parts can was put into the kingfisher's string bag and hauled up to the oak tree. Nor did he hear the muffled flapping of the bittern's wings as that bird, flying well out of spear range, landed in the top of the hickory tree that overhung the dolls' house and lowered the BONZO can with Frog inside it. Dangling in his armoured gondola, the fortuneteller removed the clothesline pulley from its branch, and silently departed with it.

The active uncle made his next non-appearance on the railway gantry that bridged the tracks, and later, when the midnight special passed the dump, the white beam of its headlight showed the clothesline pulley hanging there below the semaphores and signal lights.

All of this went on unknown to Manny Rat and the guards on duty, who, having sampled the punch, may have been somewhat less than fully alert. All that night the boss of the dump walked his tower and thought long thoughts of rising dogs. Night was his daytime, and in his present state of mind the coming dawn called up a bright and nameless dread. He thought of sunlight on those whispering leaves, and shuddered, covering his eyes with his paws.

So he did not see, low on the horizon just before the dawn, the star that for the first time rose to trace its circle in the end-of-summer sky. And had he seen it he would not have known its name, he who turned from sun and moon and stars alike. Sirius it was, the brightest star in all the heavens, that flashed its fire on the paling sky; Sirius, called the Dog Star, that steadily burned afar and looked down on the dolls' house and the dump.

The party and the sherry bottle had lasted through the night, but both had reached the end of their resources in the dim, blue, mists of morning. Most of the guests lay where they had fallen, replete with good cheer. A few of the gaunt, artistic rats, their burning eyes still half open, prowled hopefully among the remains of the garbage buffet. Outside the house a sleepy guard, the only one still at his post, looked on while some of the golden youth and maiden rats amused themselves by seeing how close to the edge they could ride the elephant without falling off the platform. On his tower Manny Rat dozed fitfully, his head cradled in his paws. And in the weeds below, the forage squad, their rusty tin and rotting plush still damp with night, stood and lay where Iggy had unloaded them.

The dark horizon was suffused with light, and in the dump the voices of the night grew faint, passed into silence and the dawn. The carousel was still, the gaming booths were shut. The sexton beetle snuffed out his candles, closed his show, and buried the fish head he had taken in that night. The little wizened vendor of orange peels and library paste slowly made his way home, crunching over broken glass and leaving tracks in ashes wet with dew. A train clinked sleepily on the tracks, stopped, started again, and pulled away towards the town.

'What day is it?' chirped a frazzled sparrow to his wife.

'What's the difference?' she replied. 'It's the same as all the others. Work, work, work.'

'It's a brand new day!' said a chickadee. 'Such a day, day, day!'

'Don't be a fool,' said the sparrow.

'Morning's come again!' crowed a distant rooster. 'This dunghill's mine!'

'Morning,' said the town clock. 'For good or ill, this day begins,' and it gravely struck the hour.

The oak leaves still were whispering, but behind them now another sound was heard – a tiny, rolling drumbeat, sharp with rage and growing louder, crying war. Out of the tree, his wild crest spiky with grim purpose, his wings fast flashing in the sun, burst the kingfisher. His rattling challenge rang on the startled ears of Manny Rat, but the boss of the dump had no eyes for the bird. Passing low over the watchtower, swinging and revolving at the end of a line held by the kingfisher, was the mouse child with his nutshell drum. He and his father and the frog, racing desperately against time, had figured out the installation of clockwork. Now, equipped from the spare-parts can with a motor and a pair of red tin arms, he beat a rataplan both fierce and loud, for the little drum was newly headed with tin.

The child's eyes briefly met the furious gaze of Manny Rat, but any fine and ringing words rehearsed for this moment had vanished from his mind. 'Yah, yah!' he yelled, and off he flew.

Manny Rat leaped up, but not quite high enough, and fell back cursing. 'Iggy!' he shrieked. 'Guards!'

The lone guard on the platform whirled and flung his spear, but the kingfisher dodged cleverly and let it whistle by him, then hauled the child up short and turned for a second pass over the dolls' house. The guard ran to the rack for another spear, but before he reached it the bittern was upon him, his little yellow-spectacle eyes blazing, a large rock clenched in his feet. OONG, BONK, CHOONG! The dolls' house echoed to the blows, and the guard lay on the platform, pounded nearly flat.

The golden youths and maidens screamed and ran for shelter. Manny Rat, half mad with rage, had almost gained the spear rack when he turned and saw the kingfisher, who seemed all beak, coming at him like an arrow from a bow. He threw himself flat on the platform, felt the rush of fiercely beating wings, and received a resounding whack on the back of his head from the mouse child's tin feet. 'Ours!' said the child passionately. 'Our territory!' and was gone again.

Leaving all dignity behind him, Manny Rat dived through a window into the dolls' house, scattering startled guests all around him, then very cautiously lifted up his head and looked out in time to see the elephant being carried off in the string bag by the bittern. As the outcries of the company subsided he heard again the whispering of the oak leaves and the steady war beat of the nutshell drum. The dead guard lay on the platform, his whiskers stirring lightly in the morning breeze. A shadow passed over the body, there was a heavy flapping, a thump on the roof and the bittern settled himself into place on the tower. The rats inside all held their breath and waited. A heavy stone bounced off the platform, and the house shook slightly. 'Higher and a little to the left,' said the bittern.

Manny Rat peeped carefully from the window and saw nothing. 'Iggy!' he whispered.

'What?' said his lieutenant from the other side of the room. One of the lithe young theatrical-beauty rats had thrown herself into his arms at the first sign of danger, and he was well contented with his work.

'Don't ask me what!' hissed his master. 'Look out of your window and see what they're doing now.'

Iggy disentangled himself from the distressed beauty, put his head out of the window, caught the second stone full in the face, and fell back lifeless. The ladies recommenced their screaming.

'That's it,' called the bittern to the oak tree. 'You've got the range now.'

'Very good,' said Frog, and sent another rock whistling through the window. The catapult he employed for the purpose was the mouse father. He had been reassembled and specially modified, the hind legs of the long-departed tin donkey now replacing his arms in such a way that their kicking action made him an effective weapon. In order that the force of his motion might not hurl him from the tree, he had been lashed securely to a makeshift platform tied to a crotch of the oak. Beside the father was the seal, the rod in her nose turning slowly as she winched up a bagful of rocks from the kingfisher on the ground below. The spare-parts can stood on the platform, its contents scattered all around it: there were a beer-can opener, a pair of miniature pliers, a little screwdriver, a sardine-can key, and a tangle of fine copper wire; an array of clockwork jumbled together with the tools indicated many choices of action open to the father and son, from string climbing to fiddle playing. The kingfisher's hooks and lines completed the total of the little group's equipment. The father had asked to have the good-luck coin near him, and it lay there now, its uppermost side proclaiming silently: YOUR LUCKY DAY IS . . . The elephant, still without a word, stood near, awaiting her part in the action, and next to her was the mouse child, drumming as regularly as the frog could wind him. Having worked out with his father the strategy to be followed in the coming hours, he was now content to be a drummer boy until the battle should be won.

'We can't keep them inside indefinitely,' said the father as he hurled another stone at the enemy. 'Manny Rat's no coward, and he'll find some way of striking back in a matter of minutes.' A squawk from the bittern attested to the truth of his observation. Manny Rat had gnawed a hole in the roof and attempted an attack from the rear, but was put down again quickly.

'We'll move as fast as we can,' said Frog. He watched through the leaves as the kingfisher flew to the bottom of the pole and attached lines to the windups of the forage squad. The other ends of the lines were made fast to the crossbar of a capstan fashioned from two strong sticks and mounted by Frog on the platform. Now he hitched the elephant to the crossbar and wound her up. Round and round she walked turning the bar, and the foragers were dragged through the weeds to rise swaying up through the leaves to the platform. Next, Frog picked up a bundle of coiled lines and hooks, and stepped into the BONZO can as the breathless kingfisher returned, picked up the can's towing bridle, and took off.

'RATS!' bellowed the airborne fortune-teller as he approached the dolls' house, the empty canvas fingers of his glove sticking up out of the can. 'RATS, HEAR THIS!' The angry murmur in the house subsided, and the frog continued. 'RATS, THE HAND OF FATE IS UPON YOU,' he boomed. 'RESISTANCE IS USELESS. ALL IS LOST. DO NOT STIR.'

The can was lowered to the dolls' house roof and the frog stepped out, while the kingfisher appropriated the poisoned-spear arsenal and with the bittern patrolled the doors and windows to ensure the fortune-teller's safety. Having made certain that the roof was strongly fastened, Frog secured four doubled lines to its corners with large fishhooks, setting them deep into the wood. A fifth line was attached to the porch, and then Manny Rat, fuming inside the house, saw the little black-and-white dog on the BONZO can glide upwards past the window as the frog took off again. 'A dog shall rise,' he whimpered, and was sick at heart. Not yet ready to give up the fight, however, he crept to the window, saw the lines trailing from the roof, and saw what Frog was doing at that moment on the railway gantry. He snarled defiantly and went to work with his teeth again, this time gnawing at the floor.

In the tree the mouse child, the seal, the elephant, and the ex-forage-squad windups waited, silent while the minutes passed, until they heard the whistle of a freight approaching on the tracks. 'Now is the time,' the child said, 'and where is Uncle Frog?'

'Here,' answered the panting Frog as he landed on the platform. With the kingfisher's help he made fast all his lines to the capstan bar and hitched the ex-foragers to it in tandem rows, the elephant at their head. The danceless bear, the roarless lion, the lame, blind, mouldy goat, and all the others took their places and felt their springs wound tight. The freight train whistle blew again, much closer this time, and they heard the clacking on the rails. 'Now!' said Frog.

The battered toys strained at the capstan; the lines ran through the creaking clothesline pulley on the railway gantry, drew taut, and quivered as the fishhooks dug into the dolls' house roof. The platform in the oak tree lifted slightly, but the lashings held; the crossbar went around, and the lines, inwinding slowly, climbed row on row the stick that was the capstan drum. 'It's coming!' said the frog, and put his shoulder to the bar. The bittern, still on duty at the watchtower, gripped the parapet more tightly with his feet and flapped his wings to keep his balance as the dolls' house slid across its platform towards the railway tracks. It tilted off the edge and swung in a long arc to the gantry, accompanied by one collective wail from all the rats within. Now the house was hanging from the clothesline pulley, poised directly over the tracks as the engine of the freight train passed beneath it.

'RATS, FAREWELL!' roared Frog, and hauled away on the trip line fastened to the dolls' house porch. 'JUMP, RATS!' he commanded. The house dipped sharply, flags and bunting fluttering in the freight train's passing. The bittern flew up off the tower, and rats poured out of all the dolls' house doors and windows, thumping to the roofs of the boxcars rattling below them.

Picking themselves up in amazement, the cream of rat society – all the grizzled fighters and their wives, the beauties and the gentlemen, the dowagers, the gaunt artistic rats, and hustlers and the bravos and the golden youth – all stood on the boxcar roofs and watched the dump recede along the curving track and vanish in the distance and the haze of autumn.

The bluejay, arriving later on the scene than was his

wont, had missed the main part of the action, and although confused, was still concise: 'RATS RAILROADED,' he informed the world at large, and let it go at that.

'Now,' said Frog, when the elation of the party in the oak tree had quieted a little, 'we must return the dolls' house to the platform, and let us not forget to nail it down as quickly

as we can.' The bittern and the kingfisher took off immediately and set to work.

'We've done it!' said the father. 'We have endured and we have fought and we have won our territory!'

'Have you indeed!' said a quiet voice below them. Manny Rat, a poisoned spear in one paw, climbed wearily up to the platform and looked around him at the little group.

'We almost won!' said the mouse child. His courage now at last gave way, and he began to cry.

'Almost!' whispered the father. 'Good-bye, my little son!' The elephant stood behind him, and he felt her eyes upon him. Silently he said good-bye to her, and silently received her answer, as Manny Rat picked up the beer-can opener and moved towards the child.

In that moment Frog, noting that all the catapult stones were gone, seized the first object within reach, the good-luck coin. Holding down the father's donkey-leg arms, he laid the coin on them and quickly wound him up.

'Hold me back!' the father whispered. 'Don't let go yet!'

For the first time that day, Manny Rat found something to laugh at. 'Hold him back!' he shouted gleefully. He crossed the platform to the father, and looked down at him where he leaned back against the branch that he was lashed to. 'Yes, hold the hero back!' said Manny Rat. 'He mustn't hurt me!' Then he snarled, and brought his face and the beer-can opener close to the father. 'Smashing you and that brat of yours won't satisfy me now,' he said. 'I won't rest content until every blasted wheel and gear and every little trashy piece of your tin is scattered far and wide. Then let us see whether you or Manny Rat shall fall!'

The father's eyes were on the coin before him. 'YOU WILL SUCCEED,' it said with silent letters. He felt the point of the beer-can opener in his tin, and saw the eyes of Manny Rat fixed on his own. 'Let go!' he said to Frog. The spring's coiled power was released, the donkey legs flew up, the brass coin caught Manny Rat squarely in the mouth, knocked out his teeth, and flung him headlong from the platform. The kingfisher and the bittern, returning to the oak tree, saw him bump from branch to branch, scattering leaves and teeth about him in his fall to earth.

There was a silence in the tree. Then from below there came a rending wail, a chilling cry of pure despair. 'No teef!' wept Manny Rat. 'I am finished! I am done! No teef at all! No teef at all!' And off into the dump he took his broken spirit, his aching bones, and the good-luck coin that had undone him.

The completeness, the overwhelming finality of their victory left everyone speechless in the oak tree. Then a tinny giggle broke out from the lame, blind, mouldy goat. A three-legged bear chuckled rustily, then began to roar with laughter. One by one the others joined in, until all the windups and the frog, the kingfisher, and the bittern whooped with hysterical mirth that sent the echoes leaping on the rubbish mountains, ringing from the tin-can slopes.

Startled swallows heard, and flew up from the wires along the tracks like notes of music winging from their staves. All the dump too, from the valley of the rubbish fires to the midway and the silent carousel, heard that laughter and knew that Manny Rat had fallen.

Gradually, squeak by squeak, rattle by rattle, gasp by gasp, the din subsided, and there was silence again. The elephant, still harnessed to the capstan at the head of the forage squad, was facing the mouse father's back, and her one eye shone with a curious brilliance. A rusty whirring sounded in her works as the last unwinding coil of her spring released itself. She moved the capstan bar a creaking inch, and came into the father's field of vision. She tried to speak, was overcome by emotion, then tried again. 'Well

done, sir!' she burst out, then sobbed so hard the platform
shook and all the windups rattled with her.

'Oh, no!' the father said. 'You mustn't cry, my dear – I beg
your pardon – madam! I cannot bear to see you cry! Oh,
please be happy now! We have won at last! Our time of
suffering is over!'

'I – am so happy!' said the elephant, and then sobbed
louder than before.

'Well,' said the kingfisher. He laughed a little ratchetting
laugh, then coughed and cleared his throat. He peeled a bit
of oak bark from the branch he stood on, fussed with it, and
shifted from one foot to the other. 'Well,' he said, 'I guess
I'm off now.' But he hesitated hopefully.

'Can't you stay?' said the seal.

'Won't you stay and be our uncle, like Uncle Frog?'
begged the mouse child.

'All right,' said the kingfisher, 'I will.'

'What about me?' demanded the bittern. 'Must I take up

my lonely life in bog and marsh as if all this had never happened?'

'I had thought you wanted only to be left to yourself,' said the father.

'It's too late for that now,' replied the bittern in a voice as dismal as ever. 'Let me be an uncle.'

'We should be delighted to have you,' said the father.

'Now we'll have our house and a family with *three* uncles!' said the child happily. 'Remember when you said it was impossible, Papa? Remember I said I wanted the elephant for a mama, and you said – '

'That will do,' said his father. An awkward silence descended on the party. The mouse father and the elephant, unable to avert their eyes, continued to look directly at each other. The father tried to hum a tune, gave it up, then he and the elephant both spoke at the same time.

'You must excuse my son's impertinence,' said the father.

'And does he still?' asked the elephant. Neither heard the other, and both laughed.

'I beg your pardon,' said the father. 'Please go on. You were saying?'

'I was saying, does he still want me for a mama?' said the elephant.

'Oh, yes!' said the child. 'And I know that Papa – '

'Can speak for himself,' said his father, and forthwith lapsed into silence.

'And will he?' prompted the elephant gently.

'He hardly knows how to begin,' said the father. 'He has come to admire – more than that, to love – someone so far above him that he dare not hope she will reciprocate his feelings.'

'Ah!' said the elephant. 'Though perhaps a little taller, she has never really been above him. Were he to speak, he might find an interested listener, a listener who has seen and learned much, who knows at last the true worth of the brave and gallant gentleman she met so long ago when she was young and foolish and thought the dolls' house was hers.'

'It is yours now,' said the father.

'Only if you offer it,' said the elephant. 'You fought for it and won it.'

'I do offer it,' said the father, 'and myself, if you will have both.'

'I will,' said the elephant.

The swallows, who note by note had flown back to the wires, once more were scattered as the echoes started up anew. 'Hurrah!' shouted all the voices in the oak tree. 'Hurrah!' And once again, 'Hurrah!'

NINE

THE interrupted task of moving the dolls' house back to the platform was completed, the father's wartime donkey-leg arms were laid aside and his regular ones put on, and he and the elephant were married by the frog on the front porch that afternoon.

The wind sighed in the oak and hickory leaves; the tall weeds rustled in the yard of the abandoned cottage by the railway; a train went clattering past and hooted once. In the distance the dump glittered and smoked in the waning golden sunlight as the ex-foragers sang 'O Promise Me'. The child stood up beside his father as best man, the seal was bridesmaid, and the kingfisher and the bittern gave the elephant away as she and the mouse father swore that they would take each other, to have and to hold.

'Winding and unwinding,' intoned the frog, 'whole or broken, bright or rusty, until the end of your tin. I now pronounce you mouse and wife.'

'LATE SPORTS FINAL!' yelled the bluejay on his last trip for the day. 'DUNG BEETLES CLINCH SERIES. ROACHES SIGN NEW COACH. WINDUPS WED.'

*

The father laughed with happiness as he looked at the sun, low in the west over the dump. 'This time yesterday we had nothing,' he said. 'And today the world is ours.'

'And now for self-winding,' said the child.

'Blue,' said the elephant. 'A very pale, faded, seashore kind of blue outside, I think. Ivory trim. And inside, ivory with blue trim. Perhaps not ivory exactly — something more off-white.'

'Cream, maybe,' said the seal. 'Almost a buff, but lighter.'

'What are you talking about, my dears?' said the father.

'The house,' said his bride. 'Of course, that dreadful black paint has got to come off first.'

'And even before we get to that, we'll have to give the place a good scrubbing and air it out,' said the seal.

'Quite right,' agreed the elephant. 'I can see that you and I are going to get on very well. Between us I have no doubt that we shall soon have everything well organized. Then if the men will simply work out the means of doing what needs to be done, we can quickly put our house in good order.'

'And what about self-winding?' said the child.

'Later,' said his father. 'First things first.'

The autumn nights were colder now; the crickets chirped more slowly; other insect songs fell silent. Through the days the air quickened, the leaves changed, the wind from the fields and meadows beyond the dump was sharp with wood-smoke, and there was constant activity in the dolls' house atop the pole.

Every day two of the uncles combed the dump for supplies, while the third stood guard at the house. Either the bittern and the frog or the kingfisher and the frog were regularly to be seen returning home with salvage to be hoisted up to the platform by seal or crane. Steel wool and strong soap had been requisitioned by the elephant; sandpaper and turpentine, paint and paint brushes. Furnishings were spoken of, and glass for the windows; drapery fabrics were discussed at length. The resources of the dump were strained to the uttermost limit, and none of the males in the family knew where it would end.

All thoughts of self-winding were put aside, and the spare-parts can was in steady demand as one set of works was exchanged for another, depending on the day's activities. It was found that string-climbing clockwork produced a motion ideally suited to sandpapering paint off houses, fiddle-playing arms and motors were good for scraping, bicycle-riding mechanisms lent themselves to the stirring of colour mixtures; and all were used accordingly by the mouse and his child.

The elephant, with a little toy broom attached to her swinging trunk, swept out all the rooms. Behind her hopped the frog, wetting down the floors with a water pistol, followed by the bittern, who held the mouse father's feet while the father administered a vigorous scrubbing with brown soap. Then the frog retraced his steps for the rinsing, and the forage squad, shuffling after him with rags and fragments of sponges tied to their feet, finished the job.

The house, as it happened, was not painted completely blue, that colour being in short supply at the dump; there was only blue enough for one porch and one dormer. From the bottoms of the available paint cans, however, came other colours in all their possible combinations – crimsons and scarlets, pinks, yellows, ochres and oranges, and several shades of green. Each colour was made to go as far as it could, but no two dormers were painted the same, and every surface of the siding and all the angles of the roof were different.

Day after day the work progressed, and night after night, by the wavering light of candle stubs, the tireless windups swung from strings hauled up and lowered by the birds, while Frog hung giddily in a variety of slings and bosun's chairs, putting in the finer touches. The house was firmly nailed to the platform – the bittern saw to that, and then went on to strengthen old repairs and make new ones, until the OONG, BONK, CHOONG! of his hammering became as familiar throughout the dump as the carousel's cracked waltz.

For some time the glassless windows were as a thorn in the elephant's side, and her immediate family and all the uncles spent sleepless nights over the problem, until one day the frog, having seen a lightbulb melting in the fires, conceived a method of glass cutting by means of a red-hot wire. Flat glass was scarce in the dump, but there was an unlimited supply of bottles. Owing to variations in size, shape, and curvature, some of the resulting windows were bowed and some were not, but the amber, blue and green panes glowed like jewels when set into their frames.

Drapes and carpets were equally varied, as was the improvised furniture, but the place began to be homelike. With each dawn the Dog Star, progressively higher over the horizon as winter approached, looked down on new improvements, until at last the hammering stopped, the platform was cleared of paint cans, brushes, nails, and scraps of wood, and the elephant prounounced the dolls' house fit for occupancy.

The house's character had changed much with the fire that had wrecked it and the several stages of reconstruction that renewed it; phoenixlike, the place seemed reborn of itself. Odd bits of graceful ornament and carving still clung here and there throughout the new repairs; the crooked porches faced the weather with an easy poise; the watchtower, smartened with orange and yellow paint and finished off with a railing and a flagpole, lost its grimness. The mansard roof, however much off-true it might be, was solid as a rock, and all the wonky chimneys and dormers stood defiantly askew and felt themselves to be atop a going concern once more.

The dolls' house would never again be what it once had been; its stateliness and beauty were long gone, but something new and different emerged from the concerted efforts of the little family. When the last touches of trim had been applied and the varicoloured curtains hung at the bottle-glass windows, the house assumed a look of wild confidence and reckless bravado. Indeed, it swaggered on its perch as if it dared the world to show it and its occupants a single peril they had not seen and laughed at.

One last touch was lacking, and the spare-parts can supplied it. From the BONZO label a paper flag was made and run up the flagpole early one morning. The mouse child kept up a steady drum roll as the banner rose to the top of the staff and fluttered in the dawn breeze. The little dog on the flag smiled up at the great one fading in the sky, while at the edge of the dump, brought there by the mouse child's drum, a pathetic figure, shabby in a torn and draggled dressing gown, stood watching.

Manny Rat felt the sharpness of the coming winter in the morning air, and he shivered mumbling his toothless gums forlornly as he looked up at the heights so lately held, so briefly his, so irretrievably lost. He fingered the good-luck coin that hung now around his neck, and touching with his paw the words YOU WILL SUCCEED, he crept back slowly to his failure and his shame.

*

During the evening that followed the morning of the flag-raising, the elephant was observed to be deep in thought as she stood on the platform looking into the parlour, where the fluttering light of one dim candle alternately gained and lost its little territory in the shadows. 'Is anything troubling you, my dear?' the father asked.

'Not exactly troubling me,' said his wife. 'But the house seems to want something more, and I cannot for the life of me think what it is.'

'Another flagpole, Mama?' suggested the child.

'No,' said the elephant.

'Carpeting on the stairs?' said the seal.

'No,' said the elephant.

'Lights,' offered a quiet voice from the weeds below.

'Of course!' exclaimed the elephant. 'That's what it is! It's been so long since I lived indoors that I'd forgotten. This house used to have real lights, not just a few candle stubs.' She paused. 'Who said that?' she asked.

Frog went to the edge of the platform and looked down. 'Manny Rat,' he said.

'Ugh!' said the elephant. 'I thought we had seen the last of that loathsome creature. Send him away.' The bittern launched himself from the platform, and the sometime boss of the dump cowered abjectly in the twilight among the weeds.

'Oh, please,' he cried, 'do not send me away! I am nuffing now, and nobody! I can do no harm. Everybody laughs at Manny Rat now, and only yesterday vuh sexton beetle tried to bury me while I was napping. Have pity!'

'He really seems quite harmless now,' said the father.

'I can find some lights and put vem in for you,' said Manny Rat, 'I can figure out all kinds of fings. I am handy, and a willing worker.'

'You used to like the dark,' the mouse child said.

'No more!' said Manny Rat. 'Oh, a lonely fing is darkness!

A fearful fing, and full of hateful laughs and whispers! No good ever came of darkness! Take me in and let me work for you! How beautiful your house would be wif lights!'

'Poor wretch!' the father said. 'It's difficult not to pity him.'

'Mercy!' pleaded Manny Rat. 'Fink of it! Fink how I have helped you! Where would you be now if you had not had me to fight against! Could you have won vat victory if vere had been no Manny Rat to be defeated?'

'There is something in what he says,' agreed the frog.

'I won't have him in my house,' said the elephant.

'Really, my dear,' said her husband, 'I think that we no longer need have any fear of Manny Rat. It seems to me he's learned his lesson.'

'And if he hasn't,' said the bittern, 'I shall be very happy to hammer it into him.'

'Aside from the fact that he's a black-hearted villain, and not for a moment to be trusted,' said the elephant, 'I find him personally offensive.'

'I will take a baff,' promised Manny Rat. 'I will get a new dressing gown, and be clean and neat.'

The elephant sighed. 'It *would* be nice to have real electric lights,' she said.

So the ladder was let down for him, and Manny Rat climbed upwards once again.

*

The fallen master of the dump made good his pledge to bathe, and with the dirt, he seemed to shed the last of his pretensions. Chastened, subdued, and looking very much the humble penitent in his new dressing gown, a clean but coarse scrap of sacking, he dedicated himself to the task of bringing light to the house where he had revelled in darkness.

Having explained that results were not to be hoped for

overnight, Manny Rat began his researches at once, and applied himself to a close examination of the traces of old wiring that still remained in the dolls' house. So it was that, looking at the house from the point of view of a diligent workman rather than that of a careless master, he found many other things that wanted doing.

No job was too heavy for him, none too menial: he swept and dusted and he washed the windows; he hewed and carried, and he made repairs and improvements far beyond the modest abilities of the little windup family and the three uncles. His eye was mild, and the old demonic fire that

gleamed there once was seen no more. So meek was he, so touchingly grateful for the least kind word, that his transformation would have melted a heart of stone. The elephant, however, as impervious to his present humility as she had been to his past arrogance, made sure that he was kept under a surveillance both strict and constant.

The family being comfortably settled in the dolls' house, the mouse and his child now found leisure time in which the problem of self-winding at last might be attempted. Therefore, taking stock of their spare-parts inventory, they began to consider how it might be done.

'Not only is the solution of such a problem far beyond my abilities,' said Frog, 'but when you stop and think about it, it scarcely seems necessary. You have good friends to wind you, and all the clockwork anyone could ever want. An almost unlimited variety of activities is open to you at your convenience. Why would you want anything so tiring as constant motion?'

'You don't know what it's like to go through life the way we used to, never knowing where our next winding might be coming from,' the child said.

'It's the principle of the thing,' said the father. 'A mouse wants independence. Having fought for and won our territory, are we to be helpless to patrol its boundaries unassisted?'

The rest of the family withdrew, so that the mouse and his child might confront their problem undistracted. As father and son stood alone on the platform and looked out across the dump, the blue haze of autumn hung in the air; the leaves rattled their flaming colours in the wind; the gleaming railway tracks converged in silence on the far horizon. The marsh hawk that had brought them to their victory and their house still skimmed above his swamp. The same black crows that cawed over the snowy junkyard almost a year ago now cawed on this day too, and the sound of another winter's coming was in their voices.

'Key times Winding equals Go,' said the child.

'Go divided by Windings equals Key,' said the father.

'That isn't getting us anywhere,' said the child. 'Let's start again.'

The father stood motionless, his empty arms held out before him. The child's hands were poised above the nutshell drum that echoed to his voice. Their old, rusty motor lay on the platform before them as step by step, wheel by wheel and cog by cog they reasoned their way through the clockwork that had driven them on their journey out into the world. The sunlight faded into dusk, then darkness rose up with its myriad voice below the red glow in the sky. Night passed into silent morning and the dawn; the Dog Star flashed and glimmered. The mouse and his child, beaded with dew, watched the sun come up, and wondered when they should achieve the daring leap of discovery and the X of self-winding.

Another day passed, another night without success, and on the following morning they were no nearer to a solution than they had been when they started. Manny Rat, returning home across the silent dump with a coil of electrical wire, found them baffled and irritated, while a yawning bittern stood guard and shook his head.

'Spring times Cog . . .' said the child.

'Times Cog times Wheel,' said the father, 'and still no X.'

'Excuse me for saying so,' said Manny Rat, 'but vere are fings vat simply cannot be figured out.'

'We figured out how to get out of the pond,' said the child, 'and we figured out how to take the dolls' house away from you.'

'Oh, yes, I know,' said Manny Rat. 'No one wants to listen to a loser.' Something of his old self flashed out from his glance. 'Reasoning won't do it all,' he said. 'You have to have a feel for fings.' He put down his wire, picked up two motors from the spare-parts can, and hummed abstractedly to himself as he inspected them. 'Going and ungoing,' he murmured, and followed the coils of the steel springs caressingly with his paw. Then he sat down with the motors in his lap, and still humming, retraced the sequence of the gear trains.

Thus peacefully occupied, Manny Rat seemed completely different from his old satanic self, seemed almost another kindly uncle. Watching him, the mouse child found it difficult to believe that this was the cold-blooded murderer of windups whose fond hope only lately had been to smash him and his father.

And Manny Rat, humming placidly, as if he were indeed an uncle repairing a favourite nephew's plaything, had the same surprising thought. He stole a sidewise glance at father and son. They were not unlike him, he realized for the first time; almost they were tin caricatures of himself. In their long exposure to the weather, moss had rooted in the crevices of their tin, and now it covered them like soft green fur. Manny Rat laughed inwardly. Perhaps they were becoming animals, and he, once the most powerful animal in the dump, would turn into a toy. After all, why not? Had not their roles been totally reversed? Has not the hunted become the hunters, the losers winners? Had not they risen to his high place as he fell from it? Just such a spring as these he held had flung the coin that knocked out all his teeth. His nose quivered as he looked down at the worn brass disk that was cool against his chest, and he opened and closed his jaws as if he still could bite. Out of the corner of his eye he noted that the bittern, however sleepy, was alert and watchful. 'Ungoing into going and back again,' muttered Manny Rat, and tried to sense how energy released by one spring could be made to wind another spring.

The hours passed unheeded; twilight came again, and evening. The guardian uncles, relieving one another in regular shifts, had rotated five times through their roster. Inside the dolls' house Frog, coming off duty, lit the candles, and the blue and green and amber windows cast coloured light and shadows on the platform and the figures grouped upon it.

'And vis goes *here*,' said Manny Rat, 'and now we attach vis . . .' Almost against his will he saw his own paws find the answer that would make the triumph of his enemies complete. He had a sudden craving for treacle brittle, and sadly shook his head.

He reached for the pliers, and made connecting rods from wire so that he could rearrange the gear trains. Then he saw his paws couple the two motors together and wind one up. As the first buzzing spring uncoiled it clickingly wound up the second one, which, running down, rewound the first. Manny Rat put down the motors, stood up, and watched them wind and unwind reciprocally for several minutes. With an odd little questioning smile he picked up his screwdriver and touched the mouse father's tin with it.

'Go ahead,' said the father, and felt his senses leave him as he and the child were taken apart.

They returned to consciousness to find themselves walking, the springs inside them buzzing and clicking as they alternately expanded and contracted their coils. Manny Rat turned away without a word, dragging with him the wire he had brought home from the dump. The soft light from the windows streamed over him, and his departing shadow passed across the father and the son.

'Look, Papa!' said the child. 'He did it! We're self-winding. Oh, thank you! Thank you, Uncle Manny!'

Manny Rat dropped the wire and whirled around. 'What's vat?' he whispered.

'I didn't mean –' the child stammered. 'I meant –'

'He meant to thank you. That was all,' the father said.

Manny Rat nodded, turned his back on them, and went into the house.

So it was that the mouse and his child became self-winding, that they might unassisted walk the boundaries of the territory they had won from Manny Rat.

TEN

AFTER his remarkable success with the problem of self-winding, Manny Rat sharply accelerated his preparations for the illumination of the dolls' house. He had worked hard before, but now he seemed a driven rat. He was gone for days at a time on research expeditions in the walls of houses in the town. He found and stole miles of wire and masses of old and new equipment: miniature sockets and switches, transformers, fuses, and circuit breakers in quantities sufficient for the electrification of a dozen full-size houses.

His manner changed perceptibly; the meekness that had marked his fresh start came and went in flashes now. What was past was past, his attitude implied, and he was looking to the future. He came and went with more assurance and a brisker step, was impatient of questions and short in his answers as his preliminary work approached completion and the business of the final wiring drew near.

At last all was ready: wires had been stapled on to walls and ceilings all over the house; sockets had been screwed in place, and switches affixed. Brand-new miniature light bulbs made their gleaming appearance. A model railway transformer stood, black and mysterious, in the parlour, where it was quickly covered with a fringed cloth at the elephant's command.

'Tonight is vuh night!' said Manny Rat, and rubbed his paws together, chuckling.

'I can hardly wait for nightfall,' said the seal. 'How pretty the house will look, all lit up!'

'Yes, indeed!' said Manny Rat. 'It'll be seen for miles. I promise you vat.'

'And yet, I shouldn't like it too bright and glaring,' said the elephant. 'I'd like the effect to be warm and cosy, you know.'

'Oh, yes,' Manny Rat assured her with a toothless grin, 'it'll be warm.' And he busied himself with the materials necessary for connecting the wires from the house to those strung from pole to pole along the railway tracks.

Towards dusk, his preparations nearly finished, the ardent electrician coiled up the wire he would need and placed it on the platform. There he stopped for a lingering look at the mouse and his child, self-windingly and interminably walking their boundaries single file, prevented from going over the edge by a guard rail he had built.

The child wore his little drum as if in constant readiness to sound a call to arms. The father paced the platform with the air of a newly prosperous landowner surveying his broad acres. Behind them, wound by Frog, strolled the elephant and the seal. The elephant, now that she was Mrs Mouse, had begun to take some little pains with her appearance. Wearing a black eyepatch over the missing eye and a bright kerchief knotted over the missing ear, she achieved a look both charmingly rakish and surprisingly chic. The seal spun a gay parasol on the rod that projected upwards from her nose, and the whole little party, in their manifest contentment, mutual esteem, and pride of place, burned their image unforgettably upon the brain of Manny Rat.

Going back into the house, he went to the parlour and took from a cupboard two large, red, brass-tipped cardboard cylinders. With his beer-can opener he tore open both of them and removed a quantity of lead pellets, which he threw out of the window into the weeds below. Next, he made a careful circuit of the parlour, scattering from the cardboard cylinders a train of black powder all around the room. That done, the empty cylinders followed the pellets out of the window.

The bittern, who had been watching him with an unwinking, yellow-spectacle-eyed stare, pointed one large foot at the powder train. 'What's that you've spilled on the floor?' he asked.

'Electrical powder,' snapped Manny Rat authoritatively. 'You can't very well have electric lights wifout electrical powder.'

The bittern, born and bred in the marshes, had had no acquaintance whatever with electricity, nor did he recognize shotgun shells and gunpowder when he saw them. So he nodded wisely, pointed his beak straight up to show that he understood, and held his peace.

'Now, ven,' said Manny Rat, 'it's time to make connections.' He unwound some of the coils on the platform and led two wires in through the window, but did not connect them to the transformer as he should have. Instead, he placed the wires on the floor about an inch apart, fastened them with insulated staples, then laid the brass goodluck coin across the bare ends. The words YOUR LUCKY DAYS were facing up. Manny Rat heaped gunpowder over the coin and the wires and left the parlour, winking at the bittern as he went.

The ex-boss of the dump's conversion to goodness, auspiciously as it had begun, had suffered a jolting setback with his gift of self-winding to the mouse and his child. He had crowned the victory of those who ruined him, and the strain upon his moral fibre was too great; however black his sins had been, such high atonement was a heavy burden on him, and his mind almost gave way beneath it. Manny Rat clutched desperately at sanity, and with a sigh he gave himself again to evil.

It was in that frame of mind that he had resolved to illuminate the dolls' house in a manner very different from his original intention: he decided to burn it down.

He had avoided anything so obvious as matches, and he thoroughly enjoyed the artfulness of his deception. All he need do now was to connect the other ends of the wires to the power lines along the railway tracks. As soon as that was done, a spark would leap up in the parlour where the coin lay on the wires, the flash would ignite the gunpowder, and the dolls' house should be submitted once again to fire, this time to burn like a torch until there would be nothing left. Manny Rat giggled as he imagined the mouse and his child, charred spectres, treading endlessly the ashes of their territory. Then, slinging the loops of wire over his shoulder, he descended the string ladder, unreeling wire as he went.

It was at this point that the elephant, returning from the family promenade, came into the parlour. 'Good heavens!' she said. 'What's all this?'

'Electrical powder,' said the bittern knowledgeably. 'You can't very well have lights without it.'

'Nonsense,' said the elephant. 'Power is what you mean to say, not powder. I've seen electric lights before, and there was never any mess like this. Men simply won't clean up after themselves – that's what it amounts to. Wind me up, please, and attach my broom. That rat seems to think that just because he's got no teeth he can do pretty much as he likes,' she said grimly. 'But if he thinks he can turn my house into a dump, he's very much mistaken.'

She began to sweep up the gunpowder briskly, sending the bittern for a doll's dustpan with which to pick it up. 'What's this?' she said as she uncovered the good-luck coin and the wire ends. 'That rat's an idiot,' she said, and called the frog.

'What's the matter?' he asked.

'I don't believe that Manny Rat knows any more about electricity than I do,' said the elephant, 'and very likely less. Anybody knows that wires have to lead to something. Look, there are two nice little ends sticking out of that black box. Now, if you'll just tie these to those, the whole thing will be neater, and the lights may possibly go on. That's the way they did it in the store, I think.'

'In any case, it can do no harm to try,' said Frog. He hung the good-luck coin around his neck once more, and spliced the wires.

As Manny Rat climbed the pole up to the power lines beside the tracks he was a happier rat than he had been for a long time. Dusk had become night, the darkness caressed him lovingly, and he wished he could prolong this moment of delicious anticipation. But he dared not risk failure if he was ever to know peace of mind again.

When he reached the top of the pole he stood among the glass insulators and felt among the wires there, instinctively avoiding those great, humming, thick ones that seemed too threatening. He had gleaned useful knowledge from the local rats in his researches in the town, and with that information and his own sharp intuitions he felt reasonably safe

173

in what he was doing. The line that he selected was a relatively low-powered one that ran to the signalman's shack some distance down the tracks. He hung the string bag on the power line, climbed into it so that he should not be grounded by the pole, and scraped away the insulation. The bare copper ends of the wires he carried terminated in alligator clips, and now, holding one in each paw, he made ready to attach them.

He turned to look down at the dolls' house. The candles were lit, their soft light shining through the blue and green and amber glass, against which came and went the pacing shadows of the mouse and his child. The ex-forage-squad windups were singing some plaintive ballad the seal had taught them, and there was conversation and quiet laughter from the house as those inside it waited for the candles' glow to pale before the glories of electricity.

'Good luck, and happy burning!' said Manny Rat.

As he connected the wires there was a blinding flash, and every hair on Manny Rat stood up and crackled with blue flame. He felt a shuddering thrill as the full voltage of the power line coursed through his body and sent branching lightnings into his brain. The dolls' house blazed with light at all the windows, but the darkness swallowed Manny Rat where he lay slumped inside the string bag, his body swaying gently in the evening breeze. After a time, when he was missed, the bittern and the kingfisher came for him, and he was carried back to the parlour that he had intended to set afire. There they laid him carefully on the floor, and all the family sorrowfully stood over him.

'Poor Uncle Manny!' said the child as he paced around the room. 'I *will* call him Uncle! He made us self-winding, he made our house beautiful, and now he's dead because he gave us light.'

'He should have been content to stay in the dark,' said the blind tin goat, and his squadmates laughed.

'One can't help feeling sorry that his life was cut short like this,' the father said. 'He certainly was a changed rat at the end.'

'I shan't say that I liked him,' mourned the elephant, 'but I can't forgive myself for this. It really is too bad!'

'I don't think he's dead,' said the bittern. 'He's opening his eyes.'

'Speak to us, Uncle Manny,' said the child. 'Say something.'

Lying limp and huddled like a worn-out rag doll on the floor, Manny Rat felt life returning to him. He half sat up, and looked around him. The house, he saw, had not burned down, and he found that he was glad. 'Say vat again,' he murmured faintly.

'Say what?' asked the mouse child.

'What you called me,' said Manny Rat.

'Uncle Manny?'

Manny Rat nodded, and smiled a toothless smile, and felt the darkness that dwelt in him open to the light.

The dolls' house seemed at last complete. Every night it shone in all its brilliance like a jewel hung on the darkness at the edge of the dump, and within it all were happy and contented.

'There is, perhaps, just one more thing,' the elephant said one day. 'A small thing, really. I think our house should have a little sign.'

'What kind of sign?' said Manny Rat. 'I'll make one right away.'

'I'm not sure,' said the lady of the house. 'Something dignified and simple – you know the sort of thing I mean. Sometimes they say, 'The Gables', or 'The Elms'.

'There's only one possible name for our house,' said the child.

'And only one favourable sign,' said the father.

The BONZO label that had flown above the watchtower

175

had long since blown itself to shreds in wind and rain. But a new one was found, and Manny Rat executed a faithful copy, painting the infinite black and white dogs on the traditional orange background on an oval board, and lettering in THE LAST VISIBLE DOG quite handsomely. The effect was magical: the sign completed the place as dramatically as the eye in a painted portrait might complete a face. The house seemed visibly to grow taller, grander, and more expansive.

'That's odd,' said the elephant as she looked at the repetitively receding dogs. 'It's certainly a lovely sign, but now the house looks like an inn or a hotel.'

'A hotel,' said the pacing mouse father thoughtfully as he passed his wife in one of his regular circuits of the platform. 'Why not?' he said the next time around.

'It's the kind of place that birds would like,' the seal said. 'We'd have travellers from everywhere to talk to.'

'They could stop here every year,' said the child, 'flying

north and flying south, and we could give them shelter in the night and in the storms.'

Manny Rat lettered a little signboard that was appended to the larger one. MIGRANTS YES, it said, and the house seemed at last to have attained its full identity. The sign swung with a motion so august, and creaked with such a seasoned, veteran creak, that it and the house seemed always to have been in that predestined place, at the edge of the dump, beside the railway tracks, between the earth and sky. 'Here I am,' it said as plainly as possible. 'The Last Visible Dog, ladies and gentlemen, at your service. Shelter and good cheer for the weary traveller. Enter and be welcome!'

Thus invited, the migrants came. Day fliers setting their course by the sun saw the gay colours of the hotel by the dump and stopped to rest at nightfall. Night travellers navigating by the stars saw The Last Visible Dog shining like a lighthouse, and steered for it as darkness faded into dawn. Geese honked, passing overhead, and kept it as a landmark on their mental maps. Most of the migratory birds had already made their passage south, but late-departing warblers and thrushes landed on the platform; swallows, starlings, orioles and tanagers and soft-voiced mourning doves all praised the house and its hospitality, and promised to return on the northward trip.

All of the uncles were active as never before. Chairs and tables multiplied; red-checked tablecloths appeared, and potted plants. The place resounded to the cheerful racket of arrivals and departures. As fast as rooms were added they were occupied, and twice that fall the platform had to be enlarged.

Tin ex-forager musicians, splendidly renewed by Manny Rat, accompanied the feathered ones at evening musicales; tin clowns and jugglers entertained; tin animals did tricks; the blind goat carried trays of canapés; and the seal, when the lights were low, dimmed by Manny Rat's transformer, waggled among the tables, singing tender ballads. Father and son, pacing tirelessly among the guests, exchanged stories of travel and adventure with them, and made everyone feel thoroughly at home. The kingfisher designated himself chef, and the once-reclusive bittern became a wildly outgoing welcomer who kept a constant lookout from the tower and hailed all passing fliers. It was the elephant, however, who more than anyone else set her stamp upon the place; her immense dignity and noble carriage, charmingly relieved by the knock-about look of her black eye-patch and the pirate-style kerchief, lent the whole establishment a raffishly patrician flavour that was irresistible.

One bird told another, and by wintertime the operators of the hotel were everywhere acclaimed as matchless hosts. Indeed The Last Visible Dog was said by birds in the know to be the first and only place to roost when travelling by the dump. When the last migratory waves had passed there were still frequent visitors: chickadees, sparrows, nuthatches, and cardinals came to spend their idle hours around the tin-can stove installed in the parlour by Manny Rat. The bluejay reporter too, indefatigable in his never-ending search for news both great and small, found the parlour stove and the tray of birdseed near it to be more or less the centre of his winter rounds, and there he spent much of his time, sifting the local gossip and discussing the affairs of the day.

And yet, popular as it was then, the house had not yet reached its final flowering and full fruition. That was to come later, as the fame of the windup family and its four uncles spread in ever-widening circles. The first intimation of what was to be occurred when the Caws of Art, visiting their old friends, turned the platform into a stage, and got successfully through all three acts of *The Last Visible Dog* at The Last Visible Dog. Having achieved that, they immediately made plans for an annual drama festival that was to become one of the most eagerly anticipated events at the dump. It was to be followed, in time, by the Caws of Art Workshop, personally directed by Crow and Mrs Crow, which programme was to be rivalled in attendance only by the yearly Deep Thought Symposium, under the profound and powerful leadership of C. Serpentina. It was said by many that the strain put upon the Erector-Set crane when it hoisted the voice of swamp and pond to the platform was equalled only by the strain upon the local intellectuals when they hoisted some of his heavier thoughts, but all agreed that it was an experience not to be missed.

The residents of the dump, when they heard what was happening by the railway tracks, were for a long time apathetic; then curiosity got the better of them. Fearful and unsure at first, but growing by degrees more confident, they crept out of their alleyways and came to The Last Visible Dog to breathe the keen and bracing air of cultural revival and new thought.

The Muskrat Foundation was set up, and the first course in practical physics was taught by Manny Rat himself. He, who was to win renown as a beloved teacher and mentor to the young, never aspired to the realms of pure thought, and many of his happiest hours were spent repairing broken windups or simply tinkering around.

Frog, with the advent of the Committee for the Surveillance of Territories and the Resolution of Inter-Field Enmities, or STRIFE, as it came to be known, was elected its first chairman. He brought to that office his characteristic wisdom and foresight, and although constantly occupied with field trips, peace missions, and delegations of irate animals, he still found time, when his services were requested by customers either in doubt or in love, to tell fortunes and perform weddings.

The Fashion Forum and Homemaker's Clinic, under the joint guidance of the elephant and the seal, was an immediate success from its inception, and for several seasons eye-patches and kerchiefs were all the rage throughout the dump.

The mouse and his child, who had learned so much and had prevailed against such overwhelming odds, never could be persuaded to teach a success course. Popular demand was intense, but they steadfastly refused. The whole secret of the thing, they insisted, was simply and at all costs to move steadily ahead, and that, they said, could not be taught. They were not idle, however, and were regularly involved to some extent in all projects going forward at The Last Visible Dog.

All of that expansion and amplification, however, was still in the future. For the present, the little family, having worked long and hard to make a success of the hotel, had reached that time of year when they might relax a little and enjoy the fruits of their labours. Fall had long since gone; the hickory stood stark and bare, and brown leaves rattled on the oak. Snow lay on the roofs and chimneys of the dolls' house, and icicles hung from the eaves. The Dog Star took his wintry road across the glittering night sky, the sign swung creaking to the north wind's blast, the coloured windows threw their green and blue and amber tints across the gleaming whiteness of the platform, and the tin-can stove in the parlour glowed cosily as the year drew to a close. It was then that the family found the leisure in which to grasp for the first time the full dimensions of their happiness, and they felt themselves too small a group to contain it all.

So it was that now, on Christmas Eve, while the bells of the town rang out their carols and the night was bright with stars, the mouse and his child paced the platform with the heavily gloved Frog, listening to the jovial hub-bub of the gathering inside the house. Here they were joined by the elephant; and the three windups, guided by the guard-rail, walked around the house in companionable silence with the slowly hopping uncle. They heard the seal's voice as she led the singing in the parlour, and the windows rattled as the company joined in the chorus.

The bittern and the kingfisher had gone out weeks before with invitations, and they had diligently searched out all whose presence was essential on this night. Crow was there, and Mrs Crow, both in fine voice. Euterpe, the repertory parrot, was quoting from her favourite works while sipping a more or less moderate punch prepared by Manny Rat for the occasion. Several shrews, from both the meadow and the stream, had put aside their enmity for this evening and were very dashing with their erect, soldierly figures, their decorations and campaign ribbons. Jeb and Zeb, older muskrats now, and not so giddy as they used to be, were propounding a new much-in-little to Manny Rat, and were amazed that anyone so old should be capable of the mental leaps he made.

The triumph of the evening was, of course, the massive presence of C. Serpentina. It was with considerable trepidation that the kingfisher and the bittern had approached the voracious deep thinker to invite him to the party. The bittern had broken the ice – literally, with a rock – and the kingfisher then took the plunge and woke the celebrated voice of swamp and pond. Both birds had been suffering from colds ever since, but Serpentina was in excellent health and spirits. Reclining by a private buffet assigned especially to him, he ate steadily, while sharing with a circle of admiring starlings his latest cerebrations. It was on this very night, in fact, that the conception of the annual Deep Thought Symposium arose within his powerful mind and cast its shadow towards the future.

'I hope our guests won't miss us for a little while,' said the elephant to her husband and her son as they completed another circuit of the house. 'This night is such a happy one for me that I simply cannot take it in all at once. I find myself wanting to look at it from the outside for a moment or two. It's so difficult to believe that we have one another and all this besides!'

The father bumped against her gently as they walked, and their tin clinked softly. 'I have felt that too,' he said.

'Do you remember,' said the elephant, brushing the mouse child with her swinging trunk, 'how I sang you a lullaby when you were afraid of the great world outside the toy-shop window?'

'I remember,' said the child.

'And yet,' said the elephant, 'it was I who was afraid when I found myself alone in the world, and it was you and your papa who were brave, and rescued me. I find that very pleasant to think about.'

The mouse child cried a little. He could not help it; he was so proud of himself and so pleased with his mama.

The front door opened, sending laughter and warm air out into the frosty night, and the seal came out to them. She waggled slowly around the house with her mother and her father and her brother, spinning a new ball that Crow had brought her. 'The year's almost over,' she said. 'It was the best year I ever had. What will the coming ones be like, I wonder?'

'Better yet,' said Frog authoritatively, and together they continued around the platform, enjoying one another's company in silence.

'Good heavens!' exclaimed the father. He had been walking more and more slowly without noticing it, and now he stopped, astonished, as the reciprocally winding springs inside him, having lost a little energy each day through friction, came at last unwound. 'I'm not wound up any more!' he said.

'Well,' said Frog, 'I don't suppose anyone ever is completely self-winding. That's what friends are for.' He reached for the father's key, to wind him up again.

'Not yet,' said the father. 'It's pleasant to rest for a little while. The road has been a long one. We have been low in the summer darkness of the pond, high in the winter light here in our house; time brought a painful spring, a shattering fall, and a scattering regathered, all as you foretold.'

'And the enemy we fled at the beginning waited for us at the end,' the child said as he too came unwound, and stopped beside the frog. 'But he's not an enemy any more – he's my Uncle Manny. Will you tell our fortune again?'

'Your fortune has been made,' said Frog, 'and needs no more telling.'

They stood together, looking out into the night. The platform shook as a lonesome whistle was heard and a white light slid along the tracks past the house. A rumbling freight went slowly clanking towards the town. One of the boxcar doors stood open, and as the train rolled on, a bundle was flung out into the snow beside the roadbed. The bundle was followed by a ragged man holding a little dog in his arms. Man and dog rolled over together and rose to their feet as the train grew smaller and was swallowed in the night. The tramp brushed himself down, picked up his bundle, and with the little black-and-white dog frisking at his heels, he crunched across the starlit snow to the abandoned cottage. He walked up to the open door, then stood there, his attention caught by the dolls' house that blazed like a beacon atop its pole.

As he looked across the yard at The Last Visible Dog the town clock sent the strokes of midnight singing on the sharp, still air. 'Twelve o'clock!' it called. 'And Merry Christmas!'

'Merry Christmas, Bonzo,' said the tramp to his dog. Then he dragged a rotting wooden box over to the pole, stood on it so that he could see over the platform, and found himself looking into the faces of the mouse and his child, the elephant, the seal, and the frog.

Inside the house the bluejay reporter broke off an interview with the starlings as he heard the clock strike twelve. 'Excuse me,' he said, and stepped out on to the porch. 'EXTRA!' he yelled. 'SEASON'S GREETINGS, FEELINGS OF INTENSE GOOD WILL EXPRESSED BY ALL.' Then he squawked and drew back hastily as he saw a great, staring, whiskered face before him.

The tramp saw father and son with their family and friends about them. He saw The Last Visible Dog in all the brightness of its lights against the night; he heard the singing and the merriment inside; and he smiled and spoke to the mouse and his child for the second time.

'Be happy,' said the tramp.

Russell Hoban writes:

'I was born in Lansdale, Pennsylvania. I attended the Philadelphia Museum School, to which I transferred after five weeks at Temple University. I was in the 339th Infantry, 85th Division, Fifth Army in World War II, in the Italian campaign. After the war I lived in New York City. From 1945 to 1956 when I started freelancing as an illustrator, I had many jobs of all kinds – shipping clerk, freight handler, Western Union messenger, worked for a number of small magazines, display studios, arts studios. Before becoming an illustrator I was a television art director for five years. Then eight years of freelancing during which I fell into children's book writing. Gave up illustrating altogether in 1965 and got a job writing advertising copy for two years. Left there in 1967 to be a full time writer. I neglected to say that I was born in 1925 and I must say that I feel much older than that.'

Russell Hoban now lives in London.

On *The Mouse and his Child*: 'The idea for this book came from some friends of mine who used to keep a collection of wind-up toys that were only brought out at Christmas time when they put them under the tree. That in itself had poignancy – the toys shut up in their boxes except for those few days each year. And this particular toy has such an appealing action: the mechanism makes it vibrate so that the father turns round and round on a smooth floor, as if stepping very quickly as he circles, raising the child up and down as he goes. As the clockwork runs down he goes more and more slowly, reverses direction and often stops with the child raised high above his head. Such pathos in that little action! Many clockwork toys have that quality, but none so much as this particular one. And these toys, whether covered with fabric or plush, or with the tin exposed, are always made in two halves that never fit together exactly. I find that touching, and not irrelevant to the human situation.

'I guess it was several years after I first saw the toy that I began to write the story. But the mouse and his child were often in my mind, and eventually enough pressure built up so that I had to find the story in them. I started writing it in October 1963, worked on it while an illustrator, then during mornings, lunchtimes and evenings while working in New York as a copy-writer. It took a little over three years and four complete re-writes. And within those rewrites almost every page was revised several times. I'm a very slow worker, and it took me a long time to figure out a lot of the action. For a time I had a little fresh-water aquarium set up in the study, in which a tin can and a mechanical toy were employed as stand-ins for the Bonzo can and the mouse and his child for the pond episode. I had a dragonfly nymph in the aquarium too, and actually saw the metamorphosis, saw its wings stiffen and grow firm for its first rickety flight.'

RALPH S. MOUSE
Beverly Cleary

Ralph is a mouse – a pretty remarkable mouse. Not only has he learned to talk through years of watching television, he's also a whizz on a motorcycle. If it weren't for his hordes of cousins plaguing him for rides, he'd be perfectly content. As it is, he decides he's got to have some peace – and what better place than Ryan's school?

MAGNUS POWERMOUSE
Dick King-Smith

Magnus was a large mouse, a fearless mouse, a real power-mouse! His mother was amazed when she saw the size of her newborn infant and realized that feeding him was going to cause problems. Small wonder that she turned to a box of patent Porker Pills, used for fattening pigs, in order to feed her voracious offspring. Small wonder, too, that Magnus just grew and grew – and the bigger he grew, the more problems he caused.

THE DEMON HEADMASTER

Gillian Cross

On the first day at her new school Dinah realizes that something is horribly wrong. The children are strangely neat and well-behaved; they never run when they should walk and they never raise their voices. They even *work* during playtime. What makes them behave this way and why does Dinah find herself conforming? The answer is fear – but what is the secret of the Headmaster's control and why does he exert it?

PLAYING BEATIE BOW

Ruth Park

The game is called Beatie Bow and the children play it for the thrill of scaring themselves. But when Abigail is drawn in, the game is quickly transformed into an extraordinary, sometimes horrifying, adventure as she finds herself transported to a place that is foreign yet strangely familiar . . .

THE DRIFTWAY

Penelope Lively

The Driftway is a strange road, a travelling road, centuries old. For those who choose to hear them, there are messages along the Driftway – echoes from the past. On the run from home with his little sister, Paul thumbs a lift on Old Bill's horse-drawn cart, hoping to escape the notice of the police. But as they travel down the Driftway, the messages come and Paul begins to see something special for him in each one. A fascinating, strangely haunting novel, to set the imagination soaring.

SUMMER SWITCH

Mary Rodgers

It had all happened in a flash. One moment Ben's father was himself – the next he wasn't. He had swapped bodies with his twelve-year-old son, who didn't seem too keen to swap back! A truly amazing adventure, bursting with humour, by the author of *Freaky Friday*.

RACSO AND THE RATS OF NIMH

Jane Leslie Conly

When fieldmouse Timothy Frisby rescues young Racso, the city rat, from drowning it's the beginning of a friendship and an adventure. The two are caught up in the struggle of the Rats of NIMH to save their home from destruction. A powerful sequel to MRS FRISBY AND THE RATS OF NIMH.

MYSTERIES OF THE SEALS

Rosalind Kerven

All the fish have disappeared from the waters around the Scottish fishing village where Tom and Katie live. There is something sinister happening. The men have all been laid off and the whole village seems to be falling asleep – it's almost as if someone has put an evil spell on the place.

THE PRIME MINISTER'S BRAIN
Gillian Cross

The fiendish Demon Headmaster plans to gain control of No. 10 Downing Street and lure the Prime Minister into his evil clutches.

NICOBOBINUS
Terry Jones

Nicobobinus and his friend, Rosie, find themselves in all sorts of intriguing adventures when they set out to find the Land of the Dragons long ago. Stunningly illustrated by Michael Foreman.

SLADE
John Tully

Slade has a mission – to investigate life on Earth. When Eddie discovers the truth about Slade he gets a whole lot more adventure than he bargained for.

WOOF!
Allan Ahlberg

Eric is a perfectly ordinary boy. Perfectly ordinary that is, until the night when, safely tucked up in bed, he slowly but surely turns into a dog! Fritz Wagner's drawings illustrate this funny and exciting story superbly.

THE PRIESTS OF FERRIS
Maurice Gee

Susan Ferris and her cousin Nick return to the world of O which they had saved from the evil Halfmen, only to find that O is now ruled by cruel and ruthless priests. Can they save the inhabitants of O from tyranny? An action-packed and gripping story by the author of prize-winning THE HALFMEN OF O.